On the Banks of Plum Creek

Other titles in the

Little House on the Prairie *series:*

LAURA INGALLS WILDER

On the Banks of Plum Creek

EGMONT

EGMONT

We bring stories to life

First published in Great Britain 1958
by Methuen & Co Ltd
This edition first published in 2014 by Egmont UK Limited
The Yellow Building, 1 Nicholas Road, London W11 4AN

Text copyright © 1937 Laura Ingalls Wilder
Copyright renewed © 1965 Roger L. Macbride
Cover illustration © 2014 Jonathan Burton
Inside illustrations © 1953 Garth Williams

ISBN 978 1 4052 7217 9

www.egmont.co.uk

HarperCollins*Publishers*
1st Floor, Watermarque Building, Ringsend Road
Dublin 4, Ireland

A CIP catalogue record for this title is available from the British
Library

Printed and bound in Great Britain by the CPI Group

24114/035

Contents

I

The Door in the Ground

The dim wagon track went no farther on the prairie, and Pa stopped the horses.

When the wagon wheels stopped turning, Jack dropped down in the shade between them. His belly sank on the grass and his front legs stretched out. His nose fitted in the furry hollow. All of him rested, except his ears.

All day long for many, many days, Jack had been trotting under the wagon. He had trotted all the way from the little log house in Indian Territory, across Kansas, across Missouri, across Iowa, and a long way into Minnesota. He had learned to take his rest whenever the wagon stopped.

In the wagon Laura jumped up, and so did Mary. Their legs were tired of not moving.

'This must be the place,' Pa said. 'It's half a mile up the creek from Nelson's. We've come a good half-mile, and there's the creek.'

Laura could not see a creek. She saw a grassy bank, and beyond it a line of willow-tree tops, waving in the gentle wind. Everywhere else the prairie grasses were rippling far away to the sky's straight edge.

'Seems to be some kind of stable over there,' said Pa, looking around the edge of the canvas wagon-cover. 'But where's the house?'

Laura jumped inside her skin. A man was standing beside the horses. No one had been in sight anywhere, but suddenly that man was there. His hair was pale yellow, his round face was as red as an Indian's, and his eyes were so pale that they looked like a mistake. Jack growled.

'Be still, Jack!' said Pa. He asked the man, 'Are you Mr Hanson?'

'Yah,' the man said.

Pa spoke slowly and loudly. 'I heard you want to go West. You trade your place?'

The man looked slowly at the wagon. He looked at the mustangs, Pet and Patty. After a while he said again, 'Yah.'

Pa got out of the wagon, and Ma said, 'You can climb out and run around, girls, I know you are tired, sitting still.'

Jack got up when Laura climbed down the wagon wheel, but he had to stay under the wagon until Pa said he might go. He looked out at Laura while she ran along a little path that was there.

The path went across short sunny grass, to the edge of the bank. Down below it was the creek, rippling and glistening in the sunshine. The willow trees grew up beyond the creek.

Over the edge of the bank, the path turned and went slanting down, close against the grassy bank that rose up like a wall.

Laura went down it cautiously. The bank rose up beside her till she could not see the wagon. There was only the high sky above her, and down below her the water was talking to itself. Laura went a step farther, then one more step. The path stopped at a wider, flat place, where it turned and dropped down to the creek in stair-steps. Then Laura saw the door.

The door stood straight up in the grassy bank, where the path turned. It was like a house door, but whatever was behind it was under the ground. The door was shut.

In front of it lay two big dogs with ugly faces. They saw Laura and slowly rose up.

Laura ran very fast, up the path to the safe wagon. Mary was standing there, and Laura whispered to her, 'There's a door in the ground, and two big dogs –' She looked behind her. The two dogs were coming.

Jack's deep growl rolled from under the wagon. He showed those dogs his fierce teeth.

'These your dogs?' Pa said to Mr Hanson. Mr Hanson turned and spoke words that Laura could not understand.

But the dogs understood. One behind the other, they slunk over the edge of that bank, down out of sight.

Pa and Mr Hanson walked slowly away towards the stable. The stable was small and it was not made of logs. Grass grew on its walls and its roof was covered with growing grasses, blowing in the wind.

Laura and Mary stayed near the wagon, where Jack was. They looked at the prairie grasses swaying and bending, and yellow flowers nodding. Birds rose and flew and sank into the grasses. The sky curved very high and its rim came neatly down to the faraway edge of the round earth.

When Pa and Mr Hanson came back, they heard Pa say: 'All right, Hanson. We'll go to town tomorrow and fix up the papers. Tonight we'll camp here.'

'Yah, yah!' Mr Hanson agreed.

Pa boosted Mary and Laura into the wagon and drove out on the prairie. He told Ma that he had traded Pet and Patty for Mr Hanson's land. He had traded Bunny, the mule-colt, and the wagon-cover for Mr Hanson's crops and his oxen.

He unhitched Pet and Patty and led them to the creek to drink. He put them on their picket-lines and helped Ma make camp for the night. Laura was quiet. She did not want to play and she was not hungry when they all sat eating supper by the camp fire.

'The last night out,' said Pa. 'Tomorrow we'll be settled again. The house is in the creek bank, Caroline.'

'Oh, Charles!' said Ma. 'A dugout. We've never had to live in a dugout yet.'

'I think you'll find it very clean,' Pa told her. 'Norwegians are clean people. It will be snug for winter, and that's not far away.'

'Yes, it will be nice to be settled before snow flies,' Ma agreed.

'It's only till I harvest the first wheat crop,' said Pa. 'Then you'll have a fine house and I'll have horses and maybe even a buggy. This is great wheat country, Caroline! Rich, level land, with not a tree or a rock to contend with. I can't make out why Hanson sowed such a small field. It must have been a dry season, or Hanson's no farmer, his wheat is so thin and light.'

Beyond the firelight, Pet and Patty and Bunny were eating grass. They bit it off with sharp, pulling crunches, and then stood chewing it and looking through the dark at the low stars shining. They switched their tails peacefully. They did not know they had been traded.

Laura was a big girl, seven years old. She was too big to cry. But she could not help asking, 'Pa, did you have to give him Pet and Patty? Did you, Pa?'

Pa's arm drew her close to him in a cuddly hug.

'Why, little half-pint,' Pa said. 'Pet and Patty like to travel. They are little Indian ponies, Laura, and ploughing is too hard work for them. They will be much happier, travelling out West. You wouldn't want to keep them here, breaking their hearts on a plough. Pet and Patty will go on travelling, and with those big oxen I can break up a great big field and have it ready for wheat next spring.

'A good crop of wheat will bring us more money than we've ever had, Laura. Then we'll have horses, and new dresses, and everything you can want.'

Laura did not say anything. She felt better with Pa's arm around her, but she did not want anything except to keep Pet and Patty and Bunny, the long-eared colt.

2

The House in the Ground

Early in the morning Pa helped Mr Hanson move the wagon bows and cover on to Mr Hanson's wagon. Then they brought everything out of the dugout house, up the bank, and they packed it in the covered wagon.

Mr Hanson offered to help move the things from Pa's wagon into the dugout, but Ma said, 'No, Charles. We will move in when you come back.'

So Pa hitched Pet and Patty to Mr Hanson's wagon. He tied Bunny behind it, and he rode away to town with Mr Hanson.

Laura watched Pet and Patty and Bunny going away. Her eyes smarted and her throat ached. Pet and Patty arched their necks, and their manes and tails rippled in the wind. They went away gaily, not knowing that they were never coming back.

The creek was singing to itself down among the willows, and the soft wind bent the grasses over the top of the bank. The sun was shining and all around the wagon was clean, wide space to be explored.

The first thing was to untie Jack from the wagon wheel.

Mr Hanson's two dogs had gone away, and Jack could run about as he pleased. He was so glad that he jumped up against Laura to lick her face and made her sit down hard. Then he ran down the path and Laura ran after him.

Ma picked up Carrie and said: 'Come, Mary. Let's go look at the dugout.'

Jack got to the door first. It was open. He looked in, and then he waited for Laura.

All around that door green vines were growing out of the grassy bank, and they were full of flowers. Red and blue and purple and rosy-pink and white and striped flowers all

had their throats wide open as if they were singing glory to the morning. They were morning-glory flowers.

Laura went under those singing flowers into the dugout. It was one room, all white. The earth walls had been smoothed and whitewashed. The earth floor was smooth and hard.

When Ma and Mary stood in the doorway the light went dim. There was a small greased-paper window beside the door. But the wall was so thick that the light from the window stayed near the window.

That front wall was built of sod. Mr Hanson had dug out his house, and then he had cut long strips of prairie sod and laid them on top of one another, to make the front wall. It was a good, thick wall with not one crack in it. No cold could get through that wall.

Ma was pleased. She said, 'It's small, but it's clean and pleasant.' Then she looked up at the ceiling and said, 'Look, girls!'

The ceiling was made of hay. Willow boughs had been laid across and their branches woven together, but here and there the hay that had been spread on them showed through.

'Well!' Ma said.

They all went up the path and stood on the roof of that house. No one could have guessed it was a roof. Grass grew on it and waved in the wind just like all the grasses along the creek bank.

'Goodness,' said Ma. 'Anybody could walk over this house and never know it's here.'

But Laura spied something. She bent over and parted the grasses with her hands, and then she cried: 'I've found the stovepipe hole! Look, Mary! Look!'

Ma and Mary stopped to look, and Carrie leaned out from Ma's arm and looked, and Jack came pushing to look. They could look right down into the whitewashed room under the grass.

They looked at it till Ma said, 'We'll brush out the place and move in what we can before Pa comes back. Mary and Laura, you bring the water-pails.'

Mary carried the large pail and Laura carried the small one, and they went down the path again. Jack ran ahead and took his place by the door.

Ma found a willow-twig broom in a corner, and she brushed the walls carefully. Mary watched Carrie to keep her from falling down into the creek, and Laura took the little pail and went for water.

She hoppity-skipped down the stair-steps to the end of a little bridge across the creek. The bridge was one wide plank. Its other end was under a willow tree.

The tall willows fluttered slender leaves up against the

sky, and little willows grew around them in clumps. They shaded all the ground, and it was cool and bare. The path went across it to a little spring, where cold, clear water fell into a tiny pool and then ran trickling to the creek.

Laura filled the little pail and went back across the sunny footbridge and up the steps. She went back and forth, fetching water in the little pail and pouring it into the big pail set on a bench inside the doorway.

Then she helped Ma bring down from the wagon everything they could carry. They had moved nearly everything into the dugout when Pa came rattling down the path. He was carrying a little tin stove and two pieces of stovepipe.

'Whew!' he said, setting them down. 'I'm glad I had to carry them only three miles. Think of it, Caroline! Town's only three miles away! Just a nice walk. Well, Hanson's on his way West and the place is ours. How do you like it, Caroline?'

'I like it,' said Ma. 'But I don't know what to do about the beds. I don't want to put them on the floor.'

'What's the matter with that?' Pa asked her. 'We've been sleeping on the ground.'

'That's different,' Ma said. 'I don't like to sleep on the floor in a house.'

'Well, that's soon fixed,' said Pa. 'I'll cut some willow

boughs to spread the beds on, for tonight. Tomorrow I'll find some straight willow poles, and make a couple of bedsteads.'

He took his axe and went whistling up the path, over the top of the house and down the slope beyond it to the creek. There lay a tiny valley where willows grew thick all along beside the water.

Laura ran at his heels. 'Let me help, Pa!' she panted. 'I can carry some.'

'Why, so you can,' said Pa, looking down at her with his eyes twinkling. 'There's nothing like help when a man has a big job to do.'

Pa often said he did not know how he could manage without Laura. She had helped him make the door for the log house in Indian Territory. Now she helped him carry the leafy willow boughs and spread them in the dugout. Then she went with him to the stable.

All four walls of the stable were built of sods, and the roof was willow-boughs and hay, with sods laid over it. The roof was so low that Pa's head touched it when he stood up straight. There was a manger of willow poles, and two oxen were tied there. One was a huge grey ox with short horns and gentle eyes. The other was smaller, with fierce, long horns and wild eyes. He was bright red-brown all over.

'Hello, Bright,' Pa said to him.

'And how are you, Pete, old fellow?' he asked the big ox, slapping him gently.

'Stand back out of the way, Laura,' he said, 'till we see how these cattle act. We've got to take them to water.'

He put ropes around their horns and led them out of the stable. They followed him slowly down the slope to a level path that went through green rushes to the flat edge of the creek. Laura slowly tagged after them. Their legs were clumsy and their big feet split in the middle. Their noses were broad and slimy.

Laura stayed outside the stable while Pa tied them to the manger. She walked with him towards the dugout.

'Pa,' she asked, in a little voice, 'did Pet and Patty truly want to go out West?'

'Yes, Laura,' Pa told her.

'Oh, Pa,' she said, and there was a tremble in her voice, 'I don't think I like cattle – much.'

Pa took her hand and comforted it in his big one. He said, 'We must do the best we can, Laura, and not grumble. What must be done is best done cheerfully. And some day we will have horses again.'

'When, Pa?' she asked him, and he said, 'When we raise our first crop of wheat.'

Then they went into the dugout. Ma was cheerful,

Mary and Carrie were already washed and combed, and everything was neat. The beds were made on the willow boughs and supper was ready.

After supper they all sat on the path before the door. Pa and Ma had boxes to sit on. Carrie cuddled sleepily in Ma's lap, and Mary and Laura sat on the hard path, their legs hanging over its sharp edge. Jack turned around three times and lay down with his head against Laura's knee.

They all sat quiet, looking across Plum Creek and the willows, watching the sun sink far away in the west, far away over the prairie lands.

At last Ma drew a long breath. 'It is all so tame and peaceful,' she said. 'There will be no wolves or Indians howling tonight. I haven't felt so safe and at rest since I don't know when.'

Pa's slow voice answered, 'We're safe enough, all right. Nothing can happen here.'

The peaceful colours went all around the rim of the sky. The willows breathed and the water talked to itself in the dusk. The land was dark grey. The sky was light grey and stars prickled through it.

'It's bedtime,' Ma said. 'And here is something new, anyway. We've never slept in a dugout before.' She was laughing, and Pa laughed softly with her.

Laura lay in bed and listened to the water talking and

the willows whispering. She would rather sleep outdoors, even if she heard wolves, than be so safe in this house dug under the ground.

3

Rushes and Flags

Every morning after Mary and Laura had done the dishes, made their bed and swept the floor, they could go out to play.

All around the door the morning-glory flowers were fresh and new, springing with all their might out of the green leaves. All along Plum Creek the birds were talking. Sometimes a bird sang, but mostly they talked. Tweet, tweet, oh twitter twee twit! one said. Then another said, Chee, Chee, Chee, and another laughed, Ha ha ha, tiraloo!

Laura and Mary went over the top of their house and down along the path where Pa led the oxen to water.

There along the creek rushes were growing, and blue flags. Every morning the blue flags were new. They stood up dark blue and proud among the green rushes.

Each blue flag had three velvet petals that curved down like a lady's dress over hoops. From its waist three ruffled silky petals stood up and curved together. When Laura looked down inside them, she saw three narrow pale tongues, and each tongue had a strip of golden fur on it.

Sometimes a fat bumble-bee, all black velvet and gold, was bumbling and butting there.

The flat creek bank was warm, soft mud. Little pale-yellow and pale-blue butterflies hovered there, and alighted and sipped. Bright dragonflies flew on blurry wings. The mud squeezed up between Laura's toes. Where she stepped, and where Mary stepped, and where the oxen had walked, there were tiny pools of water in their footprints.

Where they waded in the shallow water a footprint would not stay. First a swirl like smoke came up from it and wavered away in the clear water. Then the footprint slowly melted. The toes smoothed out and the heel was only a small hollow. There were tiny fishes in the water. They were so small that you could hardly see them. Only when they went swiftly sometimes a silvery belly flashed. When Laura and Mary stood still these little fishes swarmed around their feet and nibbled. It was a tickly feeling.

On top of the water the water-bugs skated. They had tall legs, and each of their feet made a wee dent in the water. It was hard to see a water-bug; he skated so fast that before you saw him he was somewhere else.

The rushes in the wind made a wild, lonely sound. They were not soft and flat like grass; they were hard and round and sleek and jointed. One day when Laura was wading in a deep place by the rushes, she took hold of a big one to pull herself up on the bank. It squeaked.

For a minute Laura could hardly breathe. Then she pulled another. It squeaked, and came in two.

The rushes were little hollow tubes, fitted together at the joints. The tubes squeaked when you pulled them apart. They squeaked when you pushed them together again.

Laura and Mary pulled them apart to hear them squeak. Then they put little ones together to make necklaces. They put big ones together to make long tubes. They blew through the tubes into the creek and made it bubble. They blew at the little fishes and scared them. Whenever they were thirsty, they could draw up long drinks of water through those tubes.

Ma laughed when Laura and Mary came to dinner and supper, all splashed and muddy, with green necklaces around their necks and the long green tubes in their hands. They brought her bouquets of the blue flags and she put them on the table to make it pretty.

'I declare,' she said, 'you two play in the creek so much, you'll be turning to water-bugs!'

Pa and Ma did not care how much they played in the creek. Only they must never go upstream beyond the little willow valley. The creek came around a curve there. It came out of a hole full of deep, dark water. They must never go near enough to that hole, even to see it.

'Some day I'll take you there,' Pa promised them. And one Sunday afternoon he told them that this was the day.

4

Deep Water

In the dugout Laura and Mary took off all their clothes, and over their bare skins they put on old patched dresses. Ma tied on her sunbonnet, Pa took Carrie on his arm, and they all set out.

They went past the cattle path and the rushes, past the willow valley and the plum thickets. They went down a steep, grassy bank, and then across a level place where the grass was tall and coarse. They passed a high, almost straight-up wall of earth where no grass grew.

'What is that, Pa?' asked Laura; and Pa said, 'That is a tableland, Laura.'

He pushed on through the thick, tall grass, making a path for Ma and Mary and Laura. Suddenly they came out of the high grass and the creek was there.

It ran twinkling over white gravel into a wide pool, curved against a low bank where the grass was short. Tall willows stood up on the other side of the pool. Flat on the water lay a shimmery picture of those willows, with every green leaf fluttering.

Ma sat on the bank and kept Carrie with her, while

Laura and Mary waded into the pool. 'Stay near the edge, girls!' Ma told them. 'Don't go in where it's deep.'

The water came up under their skirts and made them float. Then the calico got wet and stuck to their legs. Laura went in deeper and deeper. The water came up and up, almost to her waist. She squatted down, and it came to her chin.

Everything was watery, cool, and unsteady. Laura felt very light. Her feet were so light that they almost lifted off the creek bottom. She hopped, and splashed with her arms.

'Oo, Laura, don't!' Mary cried.

'Don't go in any farther, Laura,' said Ma.

Laura kept on splashing. One big splash lifted both feet. Her feet came up, her arms did as they pleased, her head went under the water. She was scared. There was nothing to hold on to, nothing solid anywhere. Then she was standing up, streaming water all over. But her feet were solid.

Nobody had seen that. Mary was tucking up her skirts, Ma was playing with Carrie. Pa was out of sight among the willows. Laura walked as fast as she could in the water. She stepped down deeper and deeper. The water came up past her middle, up to her arms.

Suddenly, deep down in the water, something grabbed her foot.

The thing jerked, and down she went into the deep water. She couldn't breathe, she couldn't see. She grabbed and could not get hold of anything. Water filled her ears and her eyes and her mouth.

Then her head came out of the water close to Pa's head. Pa was holding her.

'Well, young lady,' Pa said, 'you went out too far, and how did you like it?'

Laura could not speak; she had to breathe.

'You heard Ma tell you to stay close to the bank,' said Pa. 'Why didn't you obey her? You deserved a ducking, and I ducked you. Next time you'll do as you're told.'

'Y-yes, Pa!' Laura spluttered. 'Oh, Pa, p-please do it again!'

Pa said, 'Well, I'll –!' Then his great laughter rang among the willows.

'Why didn't you holler when I ducked you?' he asked Laura. 'Weren't you scared?'

'I w-was – awful scared!' Laura gasped. 'But p-please do it again!' Then she asked him, 'How did you get down there, Pa?'

Pa told her he had swum under water from the willows. But they could not stay in the deep water; they must go near the bank and play with Mary.

All that afternoon Pa and Laura and Mary played in

the water. They waded and they fought water fights, and whenever Laura or Mary went near the deep water, Pa ducked them. Mary was a good girl after one ducking, but Laura was ducked many times.

Then it was almost chore time and they had to go home. They went dripping along the path through the tall grass, and when they came to the tableland Laura wanted to climb it.

Pa climbed part way up, and Laura and Mary climbed holding to his hands. The dry dirt slipped and slid. Tangled grass roots hung down from the bulging edge overhead. Then Pa lifted Laura up and set her on the tableland.

It really was like a table. That ground rose up high above the tall grasses, and it was round, and flat on top. The grass there was short and soft.

Pa and Laura and Mary stood up on top of that tableland, and looked over the grass tops and the pool to the prairie beyond. They looked all around at prairies stretching to the rim of the sky.

Then they had to slide down again to the lowland and go on home. That had been a wonderful afternoon.

'It's been lots of fun,' Pa said. 'But you girls remember what I tell you. Don't you ever go near that swimming-hole unless I am with you.'

5
Strange Animal

All the next day Laura remembered. She remembered the cool, deep water in the shade of the tall willows. She remembered that she must not go near it.

Pa was away. Mary stayed with Ma in the dugout. Laura played all alone in the hot sunshine. The blue flags were withering among the dull rushes. She went past the willow valley and played in the prairie grasses among the black-eyed Susans and goldenrod. The sunshine was very hot and the wind was scorching.

Then Laura thought of the tableland. She wanted to climb it again. She wondered if she could climb it all by herself. Pa had not said that she could not go to the tableland.

She ran down the steep bank and went across the lowland, through the tall, coarse grasses. The tableland stood up straight and high. It was very hard to climb. The dry earth slid under Laura's feet, her dress was dirty where her knees dug in while she held on to the grasses and pulled herself up. Dust itched on her sweaty skin. But at last she got her stomach on the edge; she heaved and rolled and she was on top of the tableland.

She jumped up, and she could see the deep, shady pool under the willows. It was cool and wet, and her whole skin felt thirsty. But she remembered that she must not go there.

The tableland seemed big and empty and not interesting. It had been exciting when Pa was there, but now it was just flat land, and Laura thought she would go home and get a drink. She was very thirsty.

She slid down the side of the tableland and slowly started back along the way she had come. Down among the tall grasses the air was smothery and very hot. The dugout was far away and Laura was terribly thirsty.

She remembered with all her might that she must not go near that deep, shady swimming-pool, and suddenly she turned around and hurried towards it. She thought she would only look at it. Just looking at it would make her feel better. Then she thought she might wade in the edge of it but she would not go into the deep water.

She came into the path that Pa had made, and she trotted faster.

Right in the middle of the path before her stood an animal.

Laura jumped back, and stood and stared at it. She had never seen such an animal. It was almost as long as Jack, but its legs were very short. Long grey fur bristled all over it. It had a flat head and small ears. Its flat head slowly tilted up and it stared at Laura.

She stared back at its funny face. And while they stood still and staring, that animal widened and shortened and spread flat on the ground. It grew flatter and flatter, till it was a grey fur laid there. It was not like a whole animal at all. Only it had eyes staring up.

Slowly and carefully Laura stooped and reached and picked up a willow stick. She felt better then. She stayed bent over, looking at that flat grey fur.

It did not move and neither did Laura. She wondered what would happen if she poked it. It might change to some other shape. She poked it gently with the short stick.

A frightful snarl came out of it. Its eyes sparkled mad, and fierce white teeth snapped almost on Laura's nose.

Laura ran with all her might. She could run fast. She did not stop running till she was in the dugout.

'Goodness, Laura!' Ma said. 'You'll make yourself sick, tearing around so in this heat.'

All that time, Mary had been sitting like a little lady, spelling out words in the book that Ma was teaching her to read. Mary was a good little girl.

Laura had been bad and she knew it. She had broken

her promise to Pa. But no one had seen her. No one knew that she had started to go to the swimming-hole. If she did not tell, no one would ever know. Only that strange animal knew, and it could not tell on her. But she felt worse and worse inside.

That night she lay awake beside Mary. Pa and Ma sat in the starlight outside the door and Pa was playing his fiddle.

'Go to sleep, Laura,' Ma said, softly, and softly the fiddle sang to her. Pa was a shadow against the sky and his bow danced among the great stars.

Everything was beautiful and good, except Laura. She had broken her promise to Pa. Breaking a promise was bad as telling a lie. Laura wished she had not done it. But she had done it, and if Pa knew, he would punish her.

Pa went on playing softly in the starlight. His fiddle sang to her sweetly and happily. He thought she was a good little girl. At last Laura could bear it no longer.

She slid out of bed and her bare feet stole across the cool earthen floor. In her nightgown and nightcap she stood beside Pa. He drew the last notes from the strings with his bow and she could feel him smiling down at her.

'What is it, little half-pint?' he asked her. 'You look like a little ghost, all white in the dark.'

'Pa,' Laura said, in a quivery small voice, 'I – I – started to go to the swimming-hole.'

'You did!' Pa exclaimed. Then he asked, 'Well, what stopped you?'

'I don't know,' Laura whispered. 'It had grey fur and it – it flattened out flat. It snarled.'

'How big was it?' Pa asked.

Laura told him all about that strange animal.

Pa said, 'It must have been a badger.'

Then for a long time he did not say anything and Laura waited. Laura could not see his face in the dark, but she leaned against his knee and she could feel how strong and kind he was.

'Well,' he said at last, 'I hardly know what to do, Laura.

28

You see, I trusted you. It is hard to know what to do with a person you can't trust. But do you know what people have to do to anyone they can't trust?'

'Wh-at?' Laura quavered.

'They have to watch him,' said Pa. 'So I guess you must be watched. Your Ma will have to do it because I must work at Nelson's. So tomorrow you stay where Ma can watch you. You are not to go out of her sight all day. If you are good all day, then we will let you try again to be a little girl we can trust.

'How about it, Caroline?' he asked Ma.

'Very well, Charles,' Ma said out of the dark. 'I will watch her tomorrow. But I am sure she will be good. Now back to bed, Laura, and go to sleep.'

The next day was a dreadful day.

Ma was mending, and Laura had to stay in the dugout. She could not even fetch water from the spring, for that was going out of Ma's sight. Mary fetched the water, Mary took Carrie to walk on the prairie. Laura had to stay in.

Jack laid his nose on his paws and waggled, he jumped out on the path and looked back at her, smiling with his ears, begging her to come out. He could not understand why she did not.

Laura helped Ma. She washed the dishes and made both beds and swept the floor and set the table. At dinner she sat bowed on her bench and ate what Ma set before her. Then she wiped the dishes. After that she ripped a sheet that was worn in the middle. Ma turned the strips of muslin and pinned them together, and Laura whipped the new seam, over and over with tiny stitches.

She thought that seam and that day would never end.

But at last Ma rolled up her mending and it was time to get supper.

'You have been a good girl, Laura,' Ma said. 'We will tell Pa so. And tomorrow morning you and I are going to look for that badger. I am sure he saved you from drowning, for if you had gone to that deep water you would have gone into it. Once you begin being naughty, it is easier to go on and on, and sooner or later something dreadful happens.'

'Yes, Ma,' Laura said. She knew that now.

The whole day was gone. Laura had not seen that sunrise, nor the shadows of clouds on the prairie. The morning-glories were withered and that day's blue flags were dead. All day Laura had not seen the water running in the creek, the little fishes in it, and the water-bugs skating over it. She was sure that being good could never be as hard as being watched.

Next day she went with Ma to look for the badger. In the path she showed Ma the place where he had flattened himself on the grass. Ma found the hole where he lived. It was a round hole under a clump of grass on the prairie bank. Laura called to him and she poked a stick into the hole.

If the badger was at home, he would not come out. Laura never saw that old grey badger again.

6

Wreath of Roses

Out on the prairie beyond the stable there was a long grey rock. It rose up above the waving grasses and nodding wild flowers. On top it was flat and almost smooth, so wide that Laura and Mary could run on it side by side, and so long that they could race each other. It was a wonderful place to play.

Grey-green lichens with ruffled edges grew flat on it. Wandering ants crossed it. Often a butterfly stopped to rest there. Then Laura watched the velvety wings slowly opening and closing, as if the butterfly breathed with them. She saw the tiny feet on the rock, and the feelers quivering, and even the round, lidless eyes.

She never tried to catch a butterfly. She knew that its wings were covered with feathers too tiny to see. A touch would brush off those tiny feathers and hurt the butterfly.

The sun was always warm on the big grey rock. Sunshine was always on the waving prairie grasses, and birds and butterflies in the sunshine. Breezes always blew there, warm and perfumed from the sun-warmed grasses. Far away, towards the place where the sky came down to the land, small dark things moved on the prairie. They were cattle, grazing.

Laura and Mary never went to play on the grey rock in the mornings, and they did not stay there when the sun was going down, because morning and evening the cattle went by.

They went by in a herd, with trampling hoofs and tossing horns. Johnny Johnson, the herd boy, walked behind them. He had a round red face, and round blue eyes, and pale, whitey-yellow hair. He grinned, and did not say anything. He couldn't. He did not know any words that Laura and Mary knew.

Late one afternoon Pa called them from the creek. He was going to the big rock to see Johnny Johnson bring the cattle home, and Laura and Mary could go with him.

Laura skipped with joy. She had never been so close to a herd of cattle, and she would not be afraid when Pa was there. Mary came slowly, staying close to Pa.

The cattle were already quite near. Their bawling was growing louder. Their horns tossed above the herd, and a thin, golden dust rose up around them.

'Here they come!' Pa said. 'Scramble up!' He boosted Mary and Laura on to the big rock. Then they looked at the cattle.

Red backs and brown backs, black and white and

spotted backs, surged by. Eyes rolled and tongues licked flat noses; heads tipped wickedly to gouge with fierce horns. But Laura and Mary were safe on the high grey rock, and Pa stood against it, watching.

The last of the herd was going by, when both Laura and Mary caught sight of the prettiest cow they had ever seen.

She was a small white cow. She had red ears, and in the middle of her forehead there was a red spot. Her small white horns curved inward, pointing to that red spot. And on her white side, right in the middle, there was a perfect circle of red spots as big as roses.

Even Mary jumped up and down.

'Oh look! Oh, look!' Laura shouted. 'Pa, see the cow with the wreath of roses!'

Pa laughed. He was helping Johnny Johnson drive that cow away from the others. He called back: 'Come along, girls! Help me drive her into the stable!'

Laura jumped off the rock and ran to help him, shouting, 'Why, Pa, why? Oh, Pa, are we going to keep her?'

The little white cow went into the stable, and Pa answered, 'She's our cow!'

Laura turned and ran as fast as she could. She pounded down the path and rushed into the dugout, yelling: 'Oh, Ma, Ma! Come see the cow! We've got a cow! Oh, Ma, the prettiest cow!'

Ma took Carrie on her arm and came to see.

'Charles!' she said.

'She's ours, Caroline!' said Pa. 'How do you like her?'

'But, Charles!' Ma said.

'I got her from Nelson,' Pa told her. 'I'm paying him by days' work. Nelson's got to have help, haying and harvesting. Look at her. She's a good little milch cow. Caroline, we're going to have milk and butter.'

'Oh, Charles!' said Ma.

Laura did not wait to hear any more. She turned around and ran again, as fast as she could go, along the path and down into the dugout. She grabbed her tin cup from the supper table and she rushed back again.

Pa had tied the pretty white cow in her own little stall, beside Pete and Bright. She stood quietly chewing her cud. Laura squatted down beside her and, holding the tin cup carefully in one hand, she took hold of that cow with her other hand and squeezed just as she had seen Pa do when he milked. And sure enough a streak of warm white milk went straight into the tin cup.

'My goodness! what is that child doing!' Ma exclaimed.

'I'm milking, Ma,' said Laura.

'Not on that side,' Ma told her, quickly. 'She'll kick you.'

But the gentle cow only turned her head and looked at

Laura with gentle eyes. She looked surprised, but she did not kick.

'Always milk a cow from the right side, Laura,' said Ma. But Pa said: 'Look at the little half-pint! Who taught you to milk?'

Nobody had taught Laura. She knew how to milk a cow; she had watched Pa do it. Now they all watched her. Streak after streak of milk zinged into the tin cup; then streak after streak purred and foamed, till the white foam rose up almost to the cup's brim.

Then Pa and Ma and Mary and Laura each took a big swallow of that warm, delicious milk, and what was left Carrie drank up. They felt good inside and they all stood looking at that beautiful cow.

'What is her name?' Mary asked.

Pa's big laugh rang out and he said, 'Her name is Reet.'

'Reet?' Ma repeated. 'What outlandish name is that?'

'The Nelsons called her some Norwegian name,' said Pa. 'When I asked what it meant, Mrs Nelson said it was a reet.'

'What on earth is a reet?' Ma asked him.

'That's what I asked Mrs Nelson,' said Pa. 'She kept on saying, "a reet," and I guess I looked as foolish as I felt, for finally she said, "a reet of roses." '

'A wreath!' Laura shouted. 'A wreath of roses!'

Then they all laughed till they could not laugh any more, and Pa said: 'It does beat all. In Wisconsin we lived among Swedes and Germans. In Indian Territory we lived among the Indians. Now here in Minnesota all the neighbours are Norwegians. They're good neighbours, too. But I guess our kind of folks is pretty scarce.'

'Well,' said Ma, 'we're not going to call this cow Reet, nor yet Wreath of Roses. Her name is Spot.'

7

Ox on the Roof

Now Laura and Mary had chores to do.

Every morning before the sun was up they had to drive Spot to the big grey rock to meet the herd, so that Johnny could take her with the other cattle to eat grass all day. And every afternoon they had to remember to meet the herd and put Spot in the stable.

In the mornings they ran through the dewy chill grass that wet their feet and dabbled the hems of their dresses. They liked to splash their bare feet through the grass all strung with dewdrops. They liked to watch the sun rise over the edge of the world.

First everything was grey and still. The sky was grey, the grass was grey with dew, the light was grey and the wind held its breath.

Then sharp streaks of green came into the eastern sky. If there was a little cloud, it turned pink. Laura and Mary sat on the damp, cold rock, hugging their chilly legs. They rested their chins on their knees and watched, and in the grass below them Jack sat, watching, too. But they never could see when the sky first began to be pink.

The sky was very faintly pink, then it was pinker. The colour went higher up the sky. It grew brighter and deeper. It blazed like fire, and suddenly the little cloud was glittering gold. In the centre of the blazing colour, on the flat edge of the earth, a tiny sliver of sun appeared. It was a short streak of white fire. Suddenly the whole sun bounded up, round and huge, far bigger than the ordinary sun and throbbing with so much light that its roundness almost burst.

Laura couldn't help blinking. While she blinked just once, the sky turned blue, the golden cloud vanished. The everyday sun shone over the prairie grasses where thousands of birds were flying and twittering.

In the evenings when the cattle came home, Laura and Mary always ran fast to get up on the big rock before all those heads and horns and trampling legs reached them.

Pa was working for Mr Nelson now, and Pete and Bright had no work to do. They went with Spot and the other cattle to eat grass. Laura was never afraid of gentle, white Spot, but Pete and Bright were so big that they would scare anybody.

One evening all the cattle were angry. They came bellowing and pawing, and when they reached the big rock they did not go by. They ran around it, bawling and fighting. Their eyes rolled, their horns tossed and slashed at each other. Their hoofs raised a smudge of dust and their clashing horns were frightful.

Mary was so scared that she could not move. Laura was so scared that she jumped right off the rock. She knew she had to drive Spot and Pete and Bright into the stable.

The cattle towered up in the dust. Their feet trampled and their horns slashed and they bawled. But Johnny helped to head Pete and Bright and Spot towards the stable. Jack helped, too. Jack growled at their heels and Laura ran yelling behind them. And with his big stick Johnny drove the herd away.

Spot went into the stable. Then Bright went in. Pete was going in, and Laura was not scared now, when suddenly big Pete wheeled around. His horns hooked and his tail stood up, and he galloped after the herd.

Laura ran in front of him. She waved her arms and yelled. He bellowed, and went thundering towards the creek bank.

Laura ran with all her might, to get in front of him again. But her legs were short and Pete's were long. Jack came running as fast as he could, but he only made Pete jump longer jumps.

Pete jumped right on top of the dugout. Laura saw his hind leg go down, down through the roof. She saw him sit on it. That big ox was going to fall on Ma and

Carrie, and it was Laura's fault because she had not stopped him.

He heaved and pulled his leg up. Laura had not stopped running. She was in front of Pete now and Jack was in front of him, too.

They chased Pete into the stable and Laura put up the bars. She was shaking all over and her legs were weak. Her knees kept hitting together.

Ma had come running up the path, carrying Carrie. But no harm had been done. There was only a hole through the roof where Pete's leg had come down and gone up again. Ma said it had given her a turn to see it coming down through the ceiling.

'But there's no great damage done,' she said.

She stuffed the hole full of grass, and swept out the earth that had fallen into the dugout. Then she and Laura laughed because it was funny to live in a house where a steer could step through the roof. It was like being rabbits.

Next morning while Laura was doing dishes, she saw some little dark things rolling down the whitewashed wall. They were crumbs of earth. She looked up to see where they came from, and she jumped away from there quicker than a rabbit. A big rock smashed down, and the whole ceiling poured down over it.

The sun shone down into the house and the air was full of dust. Ma and Mary and Laura choked and sneezed looking up at the sky where a ceiling should have been. Carrie sat sneezing in Ma's arms. Jack rushed in, and when he saw the sky overhead he growled at it. Then he sneezed.

'Well, that settles it,' said Ma.

'What does, Ma?' Laura asked. She thought Ma meant that something was settling the dust.

'This does,' Ma said. 'Pa will have to mend that roof tomorrow.'

Then they carried out the rock and the earth and the

bunches of hay that had fallen. Ma swept and swept again with the willow-twig broom.

That night they slept in their house, under the starry sky. Such a thing had never happened before.

Next day Pa had to stay at home to build a new roof. Laura helped him carry fresh willow boughs and she handed them to him while he wedged them into place. They put clean fresh grass thick over the willows. They piled earth on the grass. Then over the top Pa laid strips of sod cut from the prairie.

He fitted them together and Laura helped him stamp them down.

'That grass will never know it's been moved,' Pa said. 'In a few days you won't be able to tell this new roof from the prairie.'

He did not scold Laura for letting Pete get away. He only said, 'It's no place for a big ox to be running, right over our roof!'

8

Straw-Stack

When Mr Nelson's harvesting was done, Pa had paid for Spot. He could do his own harvesting now. He sharpened the long, dangerous scythe that little girls must never touch, and he cut down the wheat in the small field beyond the stable. He bound it in bundles and stacked them.

Then every morning he went to work on the level land across the creek. He cut the prairie grass and left it to dry in the sunshine. He raked it into piles with a wooden rake. He yoked Pete and Bright to the wagon, and hauled the hay and made six big stacks of it over there.

At night he was always too tired, now, to play the fiddle. But he was glad because when the hay was stacked he could plough that stubble land, and that would be the wheat-field.

One morning at daylight three strange men came with a threshing-machine. They threshed Pa's stack of wheat. Laura heard the harsh machinery noises while she drove Spot through the dewy grass, and when the sun rose chaff flew golden in the wind.

The threshing was done and the men went away with the machine before breakfast. Pa said he wished Hanson had sown more wheat.

'But there's enough to make us some flour,' he said. 'And the straw, with what hay I've cut, will feed the stock through the winter. Next year,' he said, 'we'll have a crop of wheat that will amount to something!'

When Laura and Mary went up on the prairie to play, that morning, the first thing they saw was a beautiful golden straw-stack.

It was tall and shining bright in the sunshine. It smelled sweeter than hay.

Laura's feet slid in the sliding, slippery straw, but she could climb faster than straw slid. In a minute she was high on top of that stack.

She looked across the willow tops and away beyond the creek at the far land. She could see the whole, great, round prairie. She was high up in the sky, almost as high as birds. Her arms waved and her feet bounced on the springy straw. She was almost flying, 'way high up in the windy sky.

'I'm flying! I'm flying!' she called down to Mary. Mary climbed up to her.

'Jump! Jump!' Laura said. They held hands and jumped, round and round, higher and higher. The wind blew and their skirts flapped and their sunbonnets swung at the ends of the sunbonnet strings around their necks.

'Higher! Higher!' Laura sang, jumping. Suddenly the straw slid under her. Over the edge of the stack she went, sitting in straw, sliding faster and faster. Bump! She landed at the bottom. Plump! Mary landed on her.

They rolled and laughed in the crackling straw. Then they climbed the stack, and slid down it again. They had never had so much fun.

They climbed up and slid, climbed and slid, until there was hardly any stack left in the middle of loose heaps of straw.

Then they were sober. Pa had made that straw-stack and now it was not at all as he had left it. Laura looked at Mary and Mary looked at her, and they looked at what was left of that straw-stack. Then Mary said she was going into the dugout, and Laura went quietly with her. They were very good, helping Ma and playing nicely with Carrie, until Pa came to dinner.

When he came in he looked straight at Laura, and Laura looked at the floor.

'You girls mustn't slide down the straw-stack any more,' Pa said. 'I had to stop and pitch up all that loose straw.'

'We won't, Pa,' Laura said, earnestly, and Mary said, 'No, Pa, we won't.'

After dinner Mary washed the dishes and Laura dried them. Then they put on their sunbonnets and went up the path to the prairie. The straw-stack was golden-bright in the sunshine.

'Laura! What are you doing!' said Mary.

'I'm not doing anything!' said Laura. 'I'm not even hardly touching it!'

'You come right away from there, or I'll tell Ma!' said Mary.

'Pa didn't say I couldn't smell it,' said Laura.

She stood close to the golden stack and sniffed long, deep sniffs. The straw was warmed by the sun. It smelled better than wheat kernels taste when you chew them. Laura burrowed her face in it, shutting her eyes and smelling deeper and deeper.

'Mmm!' she said.

Mary came and smelled it and said, 'Mmm!'

Laura looked up the glistening, prickly, golden stack. She had never seen the sky so blue as it was above that gold. She could not stay on the ground. She had to be high up in the blue sky.

'Laura!' Mary cried. 'Pa said we mustn't!'

Laura was climbing. 'He did not, either!' she contradicted. 'He did not say we must not climb up it. He said we must not slide down it. I'm only climbing.'

'You come right straight down from there,' said Mary.

Laura was on top of the stack. She looked down at Mary and said, like a very good little girl, 'I am not going to slide down. Pa said not to.'

Nothing but the blue sky was higher than she was. The wind was blowing. The green prairie was wide and far. Laura spread her arms and jumped, and the straw bounded her high.

'I'm flying! I'm flying!' she sang. Mary climbed up, and Mary began to fly, too.

They bounced until they could bounce no higher. Then they flopped flat on the sweet warm straw. Bulges of straw rose up on both sides of Laura. She rolled on to a bulge and it sank, but another rose up. She rolled on to that bulge, and then she was rolling faster and faster; she could not stop.

'Laura!' Mary screamed. 'Pa said –' But Laura was rolling. Over, over, over, right down that straw-stack she rolled and thumped in straw on the ground.

She jumped up and climbed that straw-stack again as fast as she could. She flopped and began to roll again. 'Come on, Mary!' she shouted. 'Pa didn't say we can't roll!'

Mary stayed on top of the stack and argued. 'I know Pa didn't say we can't roll, but –'

'Well, then!' Laura rolled down again. 'Come on!' she called up. 'It's lots of fun!'

'Well, but I –' said Mary. Then she came rolling down.

It was great fun. It was more fun than sliding. They climbed and rolled and climbed and rolled, laughing harder all the time. More and more straw rolled down with them. They waded in it and rolled each other in it and climbed and rolled down again, till there was hardly anything left to climb.

Then they brushed every bit of straw off their dresses, they picked every bit out of their hair, and they went quietly into the dugout.

When Pa came from the hay-field that night, Mary was

busily setting the table for supper. Laura was behind the door, busy with the box of paper dolls.

'Laura,' Pa said, dreadfully, 'come here.'

Slowly Laura went out from behind the door.

'Come here,' said Pa, 'right over here by Mary.'

He sat down and he stood them before him, side by side. But it was Laura he looked at.

He said, sternly, 'You girls have been sliding down the straw-stack again.'

'No, Pa,' said Laura.

'Mary!' said Pa. 'Did you slide down the straw-stack?'

'N-no, Pa,' Mary said.

'Laura!' Pa's voice was terrible. 'Tell me again, DID YOU SLIDE DOWN THE STRAW-STACK?'

'No, Pa,' Laura answered again. She looked straight into Pa's shocked eyes. She did not know why he looked like that.

'Laura!' Pa said.

'We did not slide, Pa,' Laura explained. 'But we did roll down it.'

Pa got up quickly and went to the door and stood looking out. His back quivered. Laura and Mary did not know what to think.

When Pa turned around, his face was stern but his eyes were twinkling.

'All right, Laura,' he said. 'But now I want you girls to stay away from that straw-stack. Pete and Bright and Spot will have nothing but hay and straw to eat this winter. They need every bite of it. You don't want them to be hungry, do you?'

'Oh no, Pa!' they said.

'Well, if that straw's to be fit to feed them, it MUST – STAY – STACKED. Do you understand?'

'Yes, Pa,' said Laura and Mary.

That was the end of their playing on the straw-stack.

9
Grasshopper Weather

Now plums were ripening in the wild-plum thickets all along Plum Creek. Plum trees were low trees. They grew close together, with many little scraggly branches all strung with thin-skinned, juicy plums. Around the air was sweet and sleepy, and wings hummed.

Pa was ploughing all the land across the creek, where he had cut the hay. Early before the sun came up, when Laura went to drive Spot to meet the cattle at the grey boulder, Pete and Bright were gone from the stable. Pa had yoked them to the plough and gone to work.

When Laura and Mary had washed the breakfast dishes, they took tin pails and went to pick plums. From the top of their house, they could see Pa ploughing. The oxen and the plough and Pa crawled slowly along a curve of the prairie. They looked very small, and a little smoke of dust blew away from the plough.

Every day the velvety brown-dark patch of ploughed land grew bigger. It ate up the silvery-gold stubble field beyond the hay-stacks. It spread over the prairie waves. It was going to be a very big wheat-field, and when some day

Pa cut the wheat, he and Ma and Laura and Mary would have everything they could think of.

They would have a house, and horses, and candy every day, when Pa made a wheat crop.

Laura went wading through the tall grasses to the plum thickets by the creek. Her sunbonnet hung down her back and she swung her tin pail. The grasses were crisping yellow now, and dozens of little grasshoppers jumped crackling from Laura's swishing feet. Mary came walking behind in the path Laura made and she kept her sun-bonnet on.

When they came to a plum thicket they set down their big pails. They filled their little pails with plums and emptied them into the big pails till they were full. Then they carried the big pails back to the roof of the dugout. On the clean grass Ma spread clean cloths, and Laura and Mary laid the plums on the cloths, to dry in the sun. Next winter they would have dried plums to eat.

The shade of the plum thickets was a thin shade. Sunshine flickered between the narrow leaves overhead. The little branches sagged with their weight of plums, and plums had fallen and rolled together between drifts of long grass underfoot.

Some were smashed, some were smooth and perfect, and some had cracked open, showing the juicy yellow inside.

Bees and hornets stood thick along the cracks, sucking

up the juices with all their might. Their scaly tails wiggled with joy. They were too busy and too happy to sting. When Laura poked them with a blade of grass, they only moved a step and did not stop sucking up the good plum juice.

Laura put all the good plums in her pail. But she flicked the hornets off the cracked plums with her finger nail and quickly popped the plum into her mouth. It was sweet and warm and juicy. The hornets buzzed around her in dismay; they did not know what had become of their plum. But in a minute they pushed into the crowds sucking at another one.

'I declare, you eat more plums than you pick up,' Mary said.

'I don't either any such a thing,' Laura contradicted. 'I pick up every plum I eat.'

'You know very well what I mean,' Mary said, crossly. 'You just play around while I work.'

But Laura filled her big pail as quickly as Mary filled hers. Mary was cross because she would rather sew or read than pick plums. But Laura hated to sit still; she liked picking plums.

She liked to shake the trees. You must know exactly how to shake a plum tree. If you shake it too hard, the green plums fall, and that wastes them. If you shake it too softly, you do not get all the ripe plums. In the night they will fall, and some will smash and be wasted.

Laura learned exactly how to shake a plum tree. She held its scaling-rough bole and shook it, one quick, gentle shake. Every plum swung on its stem and all around her they fell pattering. Then one more jerk while the plums were swinging, and the last ripe ones fell plum-plump! plum-plump! plump! plump!

There were many kinds of plums. When the red ones were all picked, the yellow ones were ripe. Then the blue ones. The largest of all were the very last. They were the frost plums, that would not ripen until after frost.

One morning the whole world was delicately silvered. Every blade of grass was silvery and the path had a thin sheen. It was hot like fire under Laura's bare feet, and they left dark footprints in it. The air was cold in her nose and her breath steamed. So did Spot's. When the sun came up, the whole prairie sparkled. Millions of tiny, tiny sparks of colour blazed on the grasses.

That day the frost plums were ripe. They were large, purple plums and all over their purple was a silvery thin sheen like frost.

The sun was not so hot now and the nights were chilly. The prairie was almost the tawny colour of the hay-stacks. The smell of the air was different and the sky was not so sharply blue.

Still the sunshine was warm at noon. There was no rain and no more frosts. It was almost Thanksgiving time, and there was no snow.

'I don't know what to make of it,' Pa said. 'I never saw weather like this. Nelson says the oldtimers call it grasshopper weather.'

'Whatever do they mean by that?' Ma asked him.

Pa shook his head. 'You can't prove it by me. "Grasshopper weather," was what Nelson said. I couldn't make out what he meant by it.'

'Likely it's some old Norwegian saying,' Ma said.

Laura liked the sound of the words and when she ran through the crackling prairie grasses and saw the grasshoppers jumping she sang to herself: 'Grasshopper weather! Grasshopper weather!'

10

Cattle in the Hay

Summer was gone, winter was coming, and now it was time for Pa to make a trip to town. Here in Minnesota, town was so near that Pa would be gone only one day, and Ma was going with him.

She took Carrie, because Carrie was too little to be left far from Ma. But Mary and Laura were big girls. Mary was going on nine and Laura was going on eight, and they could stay at home and take care of everything while Pa and Ma were gone.

For going-to-town, Ma made a new dress for Carrie, from the pink calico that Laura had worn when she was little. There was enough of it to make Carrie a little pink sunbonnet. Carrie's hair had been in curl-papers all night. It hung in long, golden, round curls, and when Ma tied the pink sunbonnet strings under Carrie's chin, Carrie looked like a rose.

Ma wore her hoopskirts and her best dress, the beautiful challis with little strawberries on it, that she had worn to the sugaring-dance at Grandma's, long ago in the Big Woods.

'Now be good girls, Laura and Mary,' was the last thing she said. She was on the wagon seat, with Carrie beside her. Their lunch was in the wagon. Pa took up the ox goad.

'We'll be back before sundown,' he promised. 'Hi-oop!' he said to Pete and Bright. The big ox and the little one leaned into their yoke and the wagon started.

'Goodbye, Pa! Goodbye, Ma! Goodbye, Carrie, goodbye!' Laura and Mary called after it.

Slowly the wagon went away. Pa walked beside the oxen. Ma and Carrie, the wagon, and Pa all grew smaller, till they were gone into the prairie.

The prairie seemed big and empty then, but there was nothing to be afraid of. There were no wolves and no Indians. Besides, Jack stayed close to Laura. Jack was a responsible dog. He knew that he must take care of everything when Pa was away.

That morning Mary and Laura played by the creek, among the rushes. They did not go near the swimming-hole. They did not touch the straw-stack. At noon they ate the corn dodgers and molasses and drank the milk that Ma had left for them. They washed their tin cups and put them away.

Then Laura wanted to play on the big rock, but Mary wanted to stay in the dugout. She said that Laura must stay there, too.

'Ma can make me,' Laura said, 'but you can't.'

'I can so,' said Mary. 'When Ma's not here, you have to do what I say because I'm older.'

'You have to let me have my way because I'm littler,' said Laura.

'That's Carrie, it isn't you,' Mary told her. 'If you don't do what I say, I'll tell Ma.'

'I guess I can play where I want to!' said Laura.

Mary grabbed at her, but Laura was too quick. She darted out, and she would have run up the path, but Jack was in the way. He stood stiff, looking across the creek. Laura looked too, and she screeched, 'Mary!'

The cattle were all around Pa's hay-stacks. They were eating the hay. They were tearing into the stacks with their horns, gouging out hay, eating it and trampling over it.

There would be nothing left to feed Pete and Bright and Spot in the winter-time.

Jack knew what to do. He ran growling down the steps to the foot-bridge. Pa was not there to save the haystacks; they must drive those cattle away.

'Oh, we can't! We can't!' Mary said, scared. But Laura ran behind Jack and Mary came after her. They went over the creek and past the spring. They came up on the prairie and now they saw the fierce, big cattle quite near. The long horns were gouging, the thick legs trampling and jostling, the wide mouths bawling.

Mary was too scared to move. Laura was too scared to stand still. She jerked Mary along. She saw a stick, and grabbed it up and ran yelling at the cattle. Jack ran at them, growling. A big red cow swiped at him with her horns, but he jumped behind her. She snorted and galloped. All the other cattle ran humping and jostling after her, and Jack and Laura and Mary ran after them.

But they could not chase those cattle away from the hay-stacks. The cattle ran around and around and in between the stacks, jostling and bawling, tearing off hay and trampling it. More and more hay slid off the stacks. Laura ran panting and yelling, waving her stick. The faster she ran, the faster the cattle went, black and brown and red, brindle and spotted cattle, big and with awful horns, and they would not stop wasting the hay. Some tried to climb over the toppling stacks.

Laura was hot and dizzy. Her hair unbraided and blew in her eyes. Her throat was rough from yelling, but she kept on yelling, running, and waving her stick. She was too scared to hit one of those big, horned cows. More and more hay kept coming down and faster and faster they trampled over it.

Suddenly Laura turned around and ran the other way.

She faced the big red cow coming around a hay-stack.

The huge legs and shoulders and terrible horns were coming fast. Laura could not scream now. But she jumped at that cow and waved her stick. The cow tried to stop, but all the other cattle were coming behind her and she couldn't. She swerved and ran away across the ploughed ground, all the others galloping after her.

Jack and Laura and Mary chased them, farther and farther from the hay. Far into the high prairie grasses they chased those cattle.

Johnny Johnson rose out of the prairie, rubbing his eyes. He had been lying asleep in a warm hollow of grass.

'Johnny! Johnny!' Laura screeched. 'Wake up and watch the cattle!'

'You'd better!' Mary told him.

Johnny Johnson looked at the cattle grazing in the deep grass, and he looked at Laura and Mary and Jack. He did not know what had happened and they could not tell him because the only words he knew were Norwegian.

They went back through the high grass that dragged at their trembling legs. They were glad to drink at the spring. They were glad to be in the quiet dugout and sit down to rest.

11

Runaway

All that long, quiet afternoon they stayed in the dugout. The cattle did not come back to the hay-stacks. Slowly the sun went down the western sky. Soon it would be time to meet the cattle at the big grey rock, and Laura and Mary wished that Pa and Ma would come home.

Again and again they went up the path to look for the wagon. At last they sat waiting with Jack on the grassy top of their house. The lower the sun went, the more attentive Jack's ears were. Often he and Laura stood up to look at the edge of the sky where the wagon had gone, though they could see it just as well when they were sitting down.

Finally Jack turned one ear that way, then the other. Then he looked up at Laura and a waggle went from his neck to his stubby tail. The wagon was coming!

They all stood and watched till it came out of the prairie. When Laura saw the oxen, and Ma and Carrie on the wagon seat, she jumped up and down swinging her sunbonnet and shouting, 'They're coming! They're coming!'

'They're coming awful fast,' Mary said.

Laura was still. She heard the wagon rattling loudly. Pete and Bright were coming very fast. They were running. They were running away.

The wagon came bumpity-banging and bouncing. Laura saw Ma down in a corner of the wagon box, hanging on to it and hugging Carrie. Pa came bounding in long jumps beside Bright, shouting and hitting at Bright with the goad.

He was trying to turn Bright back from the creek bank.

He could not do it. The big oxen galloped nearer and nearer the steep edge. Bright was pushing Pa off it. They were all going over. The wagon, Ma and Carrie, were going to fall down the bank, all the way down to the creek.

Pa shouted a terrible shout. He struck Bright's head with all his might, and Bright swerved. Laura ran screaming. Jack jumped at Blight's nose. Then the wagon, Ma, and Carrie flashed by. Bright crashed against the stable and suddenly everything was still.

Pa ran after the wagon and Laura ran behind him.

'Whoa, Bright! Whoa, Pete,' Pa said. He held on to the wagon box and looked at Ma.

'We're all right, Charles,' Ma said. Her face was grey and she was shaking all over.

Pete was trying to go on through the doorway into

the stable, but he was yoked to Bright and Bright was headed against the stable wall. Pa lifted Ma and Carrie out of the wagon, and Ma said, 'Don't cry, Carrie. See, we're all right.'

Carrie's pink dress was torn down the front. She snuffled against Ma's neck and tried to stop crying as Ma told her.

'Oh, Caroline! I thought you were going over the bank.' Pa said.

'I thought so, too, for a minute,' Ma answered. 'But I might have known you wouldn't let that happen.'

'Pshaw!' said Pa. 'It was good old Pete. He wasn't running away. Bright was, but Pete was only going along. He saw the stable and wanted his supper.'

But Laura knew that Ma and Carrie would have fallen down into the creek with the wagon and oxen, if Pa had not run so fast and hit Bright so hard. She crowded against Ma's hoopskirt and hugged her tight and said, 'Oh, Ma! Oh, Ma!' So did Mary.

'There there,' said Ma. 'All's well that ends well. Now, girls, help bring in the packages while Pa puts up the oxen.'

They carried all the little packages into the dugout. They met the cattle at the grey rock and put Spot into the stable, and Laura helped milk her while Mary helped Ma get supper.

At supper, they told how the cattle had got into the haystacks and how they had driven them away. Pa said they had done exactly the right thing. He said, 'We knew we could depend on you to take care of everything. Didn't we, Caroline?'

They had completely forgotten that Pa always brought them presents from town, until after supper he pushed back his bench and looked as if he expected something. Then Laura jumped on his knee, and Mary sat on the other, and Laura bounced and asked, 'What did you bring us, Pa? What? What?'

'Guess,' Pa said.

They could not guess. But Laura felt something crackle in his jumper pocket and she pounced on it. She pulled out a paper bag, beautifully striped with tiny red and green stripes. And in the bag were two sticks of candy, one for Mary and one for Laura!

They were maple-sugar-coloured, and they were flat on one side.

Mary licked hers. But Laura bit her stick, and the outside of it came off, crumbly. The inside was hard and clear and dark brown. And it had a rich, brown, tangy taste. Pa said it was hoarhound candy.

After the dishes were done, Laura and Mary each took her stick of candy and they sat on Pa's knees, outside the door in the cool dusk. Ma sat just inside the dugout, humming to Carrie in her arms.

The creek was talking to itself under the yellow willows. One by one the great stars swung low and seemed to quiver and flicker in the little wind.

Laura was snug in Pa's arm. His beard softly tickled her cheek and the delicious candy-taste melted on her tongue.

After a while she said, 'Pa.'

'What, little half-pint?' Pa's voice asked against her hair.

'I think I like wolves better than cattle,' she said.

'Cattle are more useful, Laura,' Pa said.

She thought about that a while. Then she said, 'Anyway, I like wolves better.'

She was not contradicting; she was only saying what she thought.

'Well, Laura, we're going to have a good team of horses before long,' Pa said. She knew when that would be. It would be when they had a wheat crop.

12

The Christmas Horses

Grasshopper weather was strange weather. Even at Thanksgiving, there was no snow.

The door of the dugout was wide open while they ate Thanksgiving dinner. Laura could see across the bare willow-tops, far over the prairie to the place where the sun would go down. There was not one speck of snow. The prairie was like soft yellow fur. The line where it met the sky was not sharp now; it was smudged and blurry.

'Grasshopper weather,' Laura thought to herself. She thought of grasshoppers' long, folded wings and their high-jointed hind legs. Their feet were thin and scratchy. Their heads were hard, with large eyes on the corners, and their jaws were tiny and nibbling.

If you caught a grasshopper and held him, and gently poked a green blade of grass into his jaws, they nibbled it fast. They swiftly nibbled in the whole grass blade, till the tip of it went into them and was gone.

Thanksgiving dinner was good. Pa had shot a wild goose for it. Ma had to stew the goose because there was no fireplace, and no oven in the little stove. But she made dumplings in the gravy. There were corn dodgers and mashed potatoes. There were butter, and milk, and stewed dried plums. And three grains of parched corn lay beside each tin plate.

At the first Thanksgiving dinner the poor Pilgrims had had nothing to eat but three parched grains of corn. Then the Indians came and brought them turkeys, so the Pilgrims were thankful.

Now, after they had eaten their good, big Thanksgiving dinner, Laura and Mary could eat their grains of corn and remember the Pilgrims. Parched corn was good. It crackled and crunched, and its taste was sweet and brown.

Then Thanksgiving was past and it was time to think of Christmas. Still there was no snow and no rain. The sky was grey, the prairie was dull, and the winds were cold. But the cold winds blew over the top of the dugout.

'A dugout is snug and cosy,' said Ma. 'But I do feel like an animal penned up for the winter.'

'Never mind, Caroline,' Pa said. 'We'll have a good house next year.' His eyes shone and his voice was like singing. 'And good horses, and a buggy to boot! I'll take you riding, dressed up in silks! Think, Caroline – this level, rich land, not a stone or stump to contend with, and only three miles from a railroad! We can sell every grain of wheat we raise!'

Then he ran his fingers through his hair and said, 'I do wish I had a team of horses.'

'Now, Charles,' said Ma. 'Here we are, all healthy and safe and snug, with food for the winter. Let's be thankful for what we have.'

'I am,' Pa said. 'But Pete and Bright are too slow for harrowing and harvesting. I've broken up that big field with them, but I can't put it all in wheat, without horses.'

Then Laura had a chance to speak without interrupting. She said, 'There isn't any fireplace.'

'Whatever are you talking about?' Ma asked her.

'Santa Claus,' Laura answered.

'Eat your supper, Laura, and let's not cross bridges till we come to them,' said Ma.

Laura and Mary knew that Santa Claus could not come down a chimney when there was no chimney. One day Mary asked Ma how Santa Claus could come. Ma did not answer. Instead, she asked, 'What do you girls want for Christmas?'

She was ironing. One end of the ironing-board was on the table and the other on the bedstead. Pa had made the bedstead that high, on purpose. Carrie was playing on the bed and Laura and Mary sat at the table. Mary was sorting quilt blocks and Laura was making a little apron for the rag doll, Charlotte. The wind howled overhead and whined in the stovepipe, but there was no snow yet.

Laura said, 'I want candy.'

'So do I,' said Mary, and Carrie cried, 'Tandy?'

'And a new winter dress, and a coat, and a hood,' said Mary.

'So do I,' said Laura. 'And a dress for Charlotte, and –'

Ma lifted the iron from the stove and held it out to them. They could test the iron. They licked their fingers and touched them, quicker than quick, to the smooth hot bottom. If it crackled, the iron was hot enough.

'Thank you, Mary and Laura,' Ma said. She began carefully ironing around and over the patches on Pa's shirt. 'Do you know what Pa wants for Christmas?'

They did not know.

'Horses,' Ma said. 'Would you girls like horses?'

Laura and Mary looked at each other.

'I only thought,' Ma went on, 'if we all wished for horses, and nothing but horses, then maybe –'

Laura felt queer. Horses were everyday; they were not Christmas. If Pa got horses, he would trade for them. Laura could not think of Santa Claus and horses at the same time.

'Ma!' she cried. 'There IS a Santa Claus, isn't there?'

'Of course there's a Santa Claus,' said Ma. She set the iron on the stove to heat again.

71

'The older you are, the more you know about Santa Claus,' she said. 'You are so big now, you know he can't be just one man, don't you? You know he is everywhere on Christmas Eve. He is in the Big Woods, and in Indian Territory, and far away in York State, and here. He comes down all the chimneys at the same time. You know that, don't you?'

'Yes, Ma,' said Mary and Laura.

'Well,' said Ma. 'Then you see –'

'I guess he is like angels,' Mary said, slowly. And Laura could see that, just as well as Mary could.

Then Ma told them something else about Santa Claus. He was everywhere, and besides that, he was all the time.

Whenever anyone was unselfish, that was Santa Claus.

Christmas Eve was the time when everybody was unselfish. On that one night, Santa Claus was everywhere, because everybody, all together stopped being selfish and wanted other people to be happy. And in the morning you saw what that had done.

'If everybody wanted everybody else to be happy, all the time, then would it be Christmas all the time?' Laura asked, and Ma said, 'Yes, Laura.'

Laura thought about that. So did Mary. They thought and they looked at each other, and they knew what Ma wanted them to do. She wanted them to wish for nothing but horses for Pa. They looked at each other again and they looked away quickly and they did not say anything. Even Mary, who was always so good, did not say a word.

That night after supper Pa drew Laura and Mary close to him in the crook of his arms. Laura looked up at his face, and then she snuggled against him and said, 'Pa.'

'What is it, little half-pint of sweet cider?' Pa asked, and Laura said,

'Pa, I want Santa Claus – to bring –'

'What?' Pa asked.

'Horses,' said Laura. 'If you will let me ride them sometimes.'

'So do I!' said Mary. But Laura had said it first.

Pa was surprised. His eyes shone soft and bright at them. 'Would you girls really like horses?' he asked them.

'Oh yes, Pa!' they said.

'In that case,' said Pa, smiling, 'I have an idea that Santa Claus will bring us all a fine team of horses.'

That settled it. They would not have any Christmas, only horses. Laura and Mary soberly undressed and soberly buttoned up their nightgowns and tied their nigh-cap strings. They knelt down together and said,

'Now I lay me down to sleep,
I pray the Lord my soul to keep.

If I should die before I wake
I pray the Lord my soul to take,

and please bless Pa and Ma and Carrie and everybody and make me a good girl for ever'n'ever. Amen.'

Quickly Laura added, in her own head, 'And please make me only glad about the Christmas horses, for ever'n'ever amen again.'

She climbed into bed and almost right away she was glad. She thought of horses sleek and shining, of how their manes and tails blew in the wind, how they picked up their swift feet and sniffed the air with velvety noses and looked at everything with bright, soft eyes. And Pa would let her ride them.

Pa had tuned his fiddle and now he set it against his shoulder. Overhead the wind went wailing lonely in the cold dark. But in the dugout everything was snug and cosy.

Bits of firelight came through the seams of the stove and twinkled on Ma's steel knitting-needles and tried to catch Pa's elbow. In the shadows the bow was dancing, on the floor Pa's toe was tapping, and the merry music hid the lonely crying of the wind.

13

A Merry Christmas

Next morning, snow was in the air. Hard bits of snow were leaping and whirling in the howling wind.

Laura could not go out to play. In the stable, Spot and Pete and Bright stood all day long, eating the hay and straw. In the dugout, Pa mended his boots while Ma read to him again the story called *Millbank*. Mary sewed and Laura played with Charlotte. She could let Carrie hold Charlotte, but Carrie was too little to play with paper dolls; she might tear one.

That afternoon, when Carrie was asleep, Ma beckoned Mary and Laura. Her face was shining with a secret. They put their heads close to hers, and she told them. They could make a button-string for Carrie's Christmas!

They climbed on to their bed and turned their backs to Carrie and spread their laps wide. Ma brought them her button-box.

The box was almost full. Ma had saved buttons since she was smaller than Laura, and she had buttons her mother had saved when her mother was a little girl. There were blue buttons and red buttons, silvery and goldy buttons, curved-in buttons with tiny raised castles and bridges and trees on them, and twinkling jet buttons, painted china buttons, striped buttons, buttons like juicy blackberries, and even one tiny dog-head button. Laura squealed when she saw it.

'Sh!' Ma shushed her. But Carrie did not wake up.

Ma gave them all those buttons to make a button-string for Carrie.

After that, Laura did not mind staying in the dugout. When she saw the outdoors, the wind was driving snow drifts across the bare frozen land. The creek was ice and the willow tops rattled. In the dugout she and Mary had their secret.

They played gently with Carrie and gave her everything she wanted. They cuddled her and sang to her and got her to sleep whenever they could. Then they worked on the button string.

Mary had one end of the string and Laura had the other. They picked out the buttons they wanted and strung them on the string. They held the string out and looked at it, and took off some buttons and put on others. Sometimes they took every button off, and started again. They were going to make the most beautiful button-string in the world.

One day Ma told them that this was the day before

Christmas. They must finish the button-string that day.

They could not get Carrie to sleep. She ran and shouted, climbed on benches and jumped off, and skipped and sang. She did not get tired. Mary told her to sit still like a little lady, but she wouldn't. Laura let her hold Charlotte, and she jounced Charlotte up and down and flung her against the wall.

Finally Ma cuddled her and sang. Laura and Mary were perfectly still. Lower and lower Ma sang, and Carrie's eyes blinked till they shut. When softly Ma stopped singing, Carrie's eyes popped open and she shouted, 'More, Ma! More!'

But at last she fell asleep. Then quickly, quickly, Laura and Mary finished the button-string. Ma tied the ends together for them. It was done; they could not change one button more. It was a beautiful button-string.

That evening after supper, when Carrie was sound asleep, Ma hung her clean little pair of stockings from the table edge. Laura and Mary, in their nightgowns, slid the button-string into one stocking.

Then that was all. Mary and Laura were going to bed when Pa asked them, 'Aren't you girls going to hang your stockings?'

'But I thought,' Laura said, 'I thought Santa Claus was going to bring us horses.'

'Maybe he will,' said Pa. 'But little girls always hang up their stockings on Christmas Eve, don't they?'

Laura did not know what to think. Neither did Mary. Ma took two clean stockings out of the clothes-box, and Pa helped hang them beside Carrie's. Laura and Mary said their prayers and went to sleep, wondering.

In the morning Laura heard the fire crackling. She opened one eye the least bit, and saw lamplight, and a bulge in her Christmas stocking.

She yelled and jumped out of bed. Mary came running, too, and Carrie woke up. In Laura's stocking, and in Mary's stocking, there were little paper packages, just alike. In the packages was candy.

Laura had six pieces, and Mary had six. They had never seen such beautiful candy. It was too beautiful to eat. Some pieces were like ribbons, bent in waves. Some were short bits of round stick candy, and on their flat ends were coloured flowers that went all the way through. Some were perfectly round and striped.

In one of Carrie's stockings were four pieces of that beautiful candy. In the other was the button-string. Carrie's eyes and her mouth were perfectly round when she saw it. Then she squealed, and grabbed it and squealed again. She sat on Pa's knee, looking at her candy and her button-string and wriggling and laughing with joy.

Then it was time for Pa to do the chores. He said, 'Do you suppose there is anything for us in the stable?' And Ma said, 'Dress as fast as you can, girls, and you can go to the stable and see what Pa finds.'

It was winter, so they had to put on stockings and shoes. But Ma helped them button up the shoes and she pinned their shawls under their chins. They ran out into the cold.

Everything was grey, except a long red streak in the eastern sky. Its red light shone on the patches of grey-white snow. Snow was caught in the dead grass

on the walls and roof of the stable and it was red. Pa stood waiting in the stable door. He laughed when he saw Laura and Mary, and he stepped outside to let them go in.

There, standing in Pete's and Bright's places, were two horses.

They were larger than Pet and Patty, and they were a soft, red-brown colour, shining like silk. Their manes and tails were black. Their eyes were bright and gentle. They put their velvety noses down to Laura and nibbled softly at her hand and breathed warm on it.

'Well, flutterbudget!' said Pa, 'and Mary. How do you girls like your Christmas?'

'Very much, Pa,' said Mary, but Laura could only say, 'Oh, Pa!'

Pa's eyes shone deep and he asked, 'Who wants to ride the Christmas horses to water?'

Laura could hardly wait while he lifted Mary up and showed her how to hold on to the mane, and told her not to be afraid. Then Pa's strong hands swung Laura up. She sat on the horse's big, gentle back and felt its aliveness carrying her.

All outdoors was glittering now with sunshine on snow and frost. Pa went ahead, leading the horses and carrying his axe to break the ice in the creek so they could drink.

A MERRY CHRISTMAS

The horses lifted their heads and took deep breaths and whooshed the cold out of their noses. Their velvety ears pricked forward, then back and forward again.

14

Spring Floods

In the middle of the night Laura sat straight up in bed. She never heard anything like the roaring at the door.

'Pa! Pa, what's that?' she screamed.

'Sounds like the creek,' he said, jumping out of bed. He opened the door, and the roaring came into the black darkness of the dugout. It scared Laura.

She heard Pa shouting, 'Jiminy crickets! It's raining fish-hooks and hammer handles!'

Ma said something that Laura could not hear.

'Can't see a thing!' Pa shouted. 'It's dark as a stack of black cats! Don't worry, the creek can't get this high! It will go over the low bank on the other side!'

He shut the door and the roaring was not so loud.

'Go to sleep, Laura,' he said. But Laura lay awake, listening to that roaring thundering by the door.

Then she opened her eyes. The window was grey. Pa was gone, Ma was getting breakfast, but the creek was still roaring.

In a flash Laura was out of bed and opening the door. Whoosh! Icy cold rain went all over her and took her breath away. She jumped out, into cold water pouring down her whole skin. Right at her feet the creek was rushing and roaring.

The path ended where she was. Angry water was leaping and rolling over the steps that used to go down to the footbridge. The willow clumps were drowned and tree tops swirled in yellow foam. The noise crowded into Laura's ears. She could not hear the rain. She felt it beating on her sopping-wet nightgown, she felt it striking her head as if she had no hair, but she heard only the creek's wild roaring.

The fast, strong water was fearful and fascinating. It snarled foaming through the willow tops and swirled far out on the prairie. It came dashing high and white around the bend upstream. It was always changing and always the same, strong and terrible.

Suddenly Ma jerked Laura into the dugout, asking her, 'Didn't you hear me call you?'

'No, Ma,' Laura said.

'Well, no,' said Ma, 'I suppose you didn't.'

Water was streaming down Laura and making a puddle around her bare feet. Ma pulled off her sticking-wet nightgown and rubbed her hard all over with a towel.

'Now dress quickly,' Ma said, 'or you'll catch your death of cold.'

But Laura was glowing warm. She had never felt so fine and frisky. Mary said, 'I'm surprised at you, Laura. I wouldn't go out in the rain and get all wet like that.'

'Oh, Mary, you just ought to see the creek!' Laura cried, and she asked, 'Ma, may I go out and see it again after breakfast?'

'You may not,' said Ma. 'Not while it is raining.'

But while they were eating breakfast the rain stopped. The sun was shining, and Pa said that Laura and Mary might go with him to look at the creek.

The air was fresh and clean and damp. It smelled like spring. The sky was blue, with large clouds sailing in it. All the snow was gone from the soaking wet earth. Up on the high bank, Laura could still hear the creek roaring.

'This weather beats me,' said Pa. 'I never saw anything like it.'

'Is it still grasshopper weather?' Laura asked him, but Pa did not know.

They went along the high bank, looking at the strange sights. The roaring, foaming creek changed everything. The plum thickets were only foamy brushwood in the water. The tableland was a round island. All around it the water flowed smoothly, coming out of a wide, humping river and running back into it. Where the swimming-pool had been, the tall willows were short willows standing in a lake.

Beyond them, the land that Pa had ploughed lay black and wet. Pa looked at it and said, 'It won't be long now till I can get the wheat planted.'

15

The Footbridge

Next day Laura was sure that Ma would not let her go to play in the creek. It was still roaring, but more softly. In the dugout she could hear it calling her. So Laura quietly slipped outdoors without saying anything to Ma.

The water was not so high now. It had gone down from the steps and Laura could see it foaming against the footbridge. Part of the plank was above the water.

All winter the creek had been covered with ice; it had been motionless and still, never making a sound. Now it was running swiftly and making a joyful noise. Where it struck the edge of the plank it foamed up in white bubbles and laughed to itself.

Laura took off her shoes and stockings and put them safely on the bottom step. Then she walked out on the plank and stood watching the noisy water.

Drops splashed her bare feet and thin little waves ran around them. She dabbled one foot in the swirling foam. Then down she sat on the plank and plumped both legs into the water. The creek ran strong against them and she kicked against it. That was fun!

Now she was wet almost all over, but her whole skin wanted to be in the water. She lay on her stomach and thrust her arms down on each side of the plank, deep into the fast current. But that was not enough. She wanted to be really in the roaring, joyous creek. She clasped her hands together under the plank and rolled off it.

In that very instant, she knew the creek was not playing. It was strong and terrible. It seized her whole body and pulled it under the plank. Only her head was out, and one arm desperately across the narrow plank.

The water was pulling her and it was pushing, too. It

was trying to drag her head under the plank. Her chin held on to the edge and her arm clutched, while the water pulled hard at all the rest of her. It was not laughing now.

No one knew where she was. No one could hear her if she screamed for help. The water roared loud and tugged at her, stronger and stronger. Laura kicked, but the water was stronger than her legs. She got both arms across the plank and pulled, but the water pulled harder. It pulled the back of her head down and it jerked as if it would jerk her in two. It was cold. The coldness soaked into her.

This was not like wolves or cattle. The creek was not alive. It was only strong and terrible and never stopping. It would pull her down and whirl her away, rolling and tossing her like a willow branch. It would not care.

Her legs were tired, and her arms hardly felt the plank any more.

'I must get out. I must!' she thought. The creek's roaring was in her head. She kicked hard with both her feet and pulled hard with her arms, and then she was lying on the plank again.

The plank was solid under her stomach and under her face. She lay on it and breathed and was glad it was solid.

When she moved, her head whirled. She crawled off

the plank. She took her shoes and her stockings and she climbed slowly up the muddy steps. At the door of the dugout she stopped. She did not know what to say to Ma.

After a while she went in. Just inside the door she stood still and water dripped off her. Ma was sewing.

'Where have you been, Laura?' Ma asked, looking up. Then she came quickly, saying: 'My goodness! Turn around, quick!' She began unbuttoning Laura down the back. 'What happened? Did you fall in the creek?'

'No, ma'am,' Laura said. 'I – I went in.'

Ma listened and went on undressing Laura and rubbing her hard all over with a towel. She did not say a word even when Laura had told her everything. Laura's teeth chattered, and Ma wrapped a quilt around her and sat her close to the stove.

At last Ma said: 'Well, Laura, you have been very naughty and I think you knew it all the time. But I can't punish you. I can't even scold you. You came near being drowned.'

Laura did not say anything.

'You won't go near the creek again till Pa or I say you may, and that won't be till the water goes down,' said Ma.

'No'm,' Laura said.

The creek would go down. It would be a gentle,

pleasant place to play in again. But nobody could make it do that. Nobody could make it do anything. Laura knew now that there were things stronger than anybody. But the creek had not got her. It had not made her scream and it could not make her cry.

16

The Wonderful House

The creek went down. All at once the days were warm, and early every morning Pa went to work the wheat-field with Sam and David, the Christmas horses.

'I declare,' Ma said, 'you're working that ground to death and killing yourself.'

But Pa said the ground was dry because there had not been enough snow. He must plough deep and harrow well, and get the wheat sowed quickly. Every day he was working before the sun came up and he worked till dark. Laura waited in the dark till she heard Sam and David splashing into the ford. Then she ran into the dugout for the lantern and she hurried to the stable to hold it so that Pa could see to do the chores.

He was too tired to laugh or talk. He ate supper and went to bed.

At last the wheat was sowed. Then he sowed oats, and he made the potato patch and the garden. Ma and Mary and Laura helped plant the potatoes and sprinkle little seeds in the garden-rows, and they let Carrie think she was helping.

The whole world was green with grass now; the yellow-green willow leaves were uncurling. Violets and buttercups were thick in the prairie hollows, and the sorrel's clover-like leaves and lavender blossoms were sour and good to eat. Only the wheat-field was bare and brown.

One evening Pa showed Laura a faint green mist on that brown field. The wheat was up! Each tiny sprout was so thin you could hardly see it, but so many of them all together made that misty green. Everyone was happy that night because the wheat was a good stand.

The next day Pa drove to town. Sam and David could go to town and come back in one afternoon. There was hardly time to miss Pa, and they were not even watching for him when he came home. Laura heard the wagon first, and she was the first one up the path.

Pa was sitting on the wagon seat. His face was one big shining of joy, and lumber was piled high in the wagon box behind him. He sang out, 'Here's your new house, Caroline!'

'But, Charles!' Ma gasped. Laura ran and climbed up over the wheel, up on to that pile of boards. She had never seen such smooth, straight beautiful boards. They had been sawed by machinery.

'But the wheat's hardly up yet!' Ma said.

'That's all right,' Pa told her. 'They let me have the lumber, and we'll pay for it when we sell the wheat.'

Laura asked him, 'Are we going to have a house made of boards?'

'Yes, flutterbudget,' said Pa. 'We're going to have a whole house built of sawed lumber. And it's going to have glass windows!'

It was really true. Next morning Mr Nelson came to help Pa, and they began digging the cellar for that house. They were going to have that wonderful house, just because the wheat was growing.

Laura and Mary could hardly stay in the dugout long enough to do their work. But Ma made them do it.

'And I won't have you giving your work a lick and a promise,' said Ma. So they washed every breakfast dish and put them all away. They made their bed neatly. They brushed the floor with the willow-twig broom and set the broom in its place. Then they could go.

They ran down the steps and over the footbridge, and under the willows, up to the prairie. They went through the prairie grasses and up to the top of a green knoll, where Pa and Mr Nelson were building the new house.

It was fun to watch them set up the skeleton house. The timbers stood up slender and golden-new, and the sky was very blue between them. The hammers made a gay sound. The planes cut long curly shavings from the sweet-smelling boards.

Laura and Mary hung little shavings over their ears for earrings. They put them around their necks for necklaces. Laura tucked long ones in her hair and they hung down in golden curls, just the colour she had always wanted her hair to be.

Up on the skeleton roof Pa and Mr Nelson hammered and sawed. Little blocks of wood fell down, and Laura and Mary gathered them in piles and built houses of their own. They had never had such a good time.

Pa and Mr Nelson covered the skeleton walls with slanting boards nailed on. They shingled the roof with bought shingles. Bought shingles were thin and all the same size; they were far finer shingles than even Pa could hew with an axe. They made an even, tight roof, with not one crack in it.

Then Pa laid the floor of silky-smooth boards that were grooved along the edges and fitted together perfectly. Overhead he laid another floor for the upstairs, and made the ceiling of the downstairs.

Across the downstairs, Pa put up a partition. That house was going to have two rooms! One was the bedroom, and the other was only to live in. He put two shining-clear glass windows in that room; one looking toward the sunrise and the other beside the doorway to the south. In the bedroom walls he set two more windows, and they were glass windows, too.

Laura had never seen such wonderful windows. They were in halves. There were six panes of glass in each half, and the bottom half would push up, and stay up when a stick was set under it.

Opposite the front door Pa put a back door, and outside it he built a tiny room. That was a lean-to, because it leaned against the house. It would keep out the north winds in the winter-time, and it was a place where Ma could keep her broom and mop and washtub.

Now Mr Nelson was not there and Laura asked questions all the time. Pa said the bedroom was for Ma and Carrie and him. He said the attic was for Mary and Laura, to sleep in and to play in. Laura wanted so much to see it that he stopped work on the lean-to and nailed strips of board up the wall, to make the attic ladder.

Laura skipped quickly up that ladder till her head came up through the hole in the attic floor. The attic was as big as both rooms downstairs. Its floor was smooth boards. Its slanting roof was the underside of the fresh, yellow shingles. There was a little window at each end of that attic, and those windows were glass windows!

At first Mary was scared to swing off the ladder to the

attic floor. Then she was scared to step down through the floor-hole on to the ladder. Laura felt scared, too, but she pretended she didn't. And they soon got used to getting on and off the ladder.

Now they thought the house was done. But Pa nailed black tar-paper all over the outside of the house walls. Then he nailed more boards over that paper. They were long smooth boards, one lapping over the other all up the sides of the house. Then around the windows and the door-ways Pa nailed flat frames.

'This house is tight as a drum!' he said. There was not one single crack in the roof or the walls or the floor of that house, to let in rain or cold winds.

Then Pa put in the doors, and they were bought doors. They were smooth, and far thinner than slab doors hewed with an axe, and even thinner panels were set into them above and below their middles. Their hinges were bought hinges, and it was marvellous to see them open and shut. They did not rattle like wooden hinges or let the door drag like leather hinges.

Into those doors Pa set bought locks, with keys that went into small, shaped holes, and turned and clicked. These locks had white china door knobs.

Then one day Pa said, 'Laura and Mary, can you keep a secret?'

'Oh yes, Pa!' they said.

'Promise you won't tell Ma?' he asked, and they promised.

He opened the lean-to door. And there stood a shiny-black cookstove. Pa had brought it from town and hidden it there, to surprise Ma.

On top, that cookstove had four round holes and four round lids fitted them. Each lid had a grooved hole in it, and there was an iron handle that fitted into the holes, to lift the lid by. In front, there was a long, low door. There were slits in this door, and a piece of iron would slide back and forth, to close these slits or open them. That was the draught. Under it, a shelf like an oblong pan stuck out. That was to catch ashes and keep them from dropping on the floor. A lid swung flat over this hollowed-out shelf. And on the lid were raised iron letters in rows.

Mary put her finger on the bottom row and spelled out, 'P A T. One seven seven nought.' She asked Pa, 'What's that spell, Pa?'

'It spells Pat,' Pa said.

Laura opened a big door on the side of that stove, and looked into a big square place with a shelf across it. 'Oh Pa, what's this for?' she asked him.

'It's the oven,' Pa told her.

He lifted that marvellous stove and set it in the living-room, and put up the stovepipe. Piece by piece, the stovepipe went up through the ceiling and the attic and through a hole he sawed in the roof. Then Pa climbed on to the roof and he set a larger tin pipe over the stovepipe. The tin pipe had a spread-out, flat bottom that covered the hole in the roof. Not a drop of rain could run down the stovepipe into the new house.

That was a prairie chimney.

'Well, it's done,' Pa said. 'Even to a prairie chimney.'

There was nothing more that a house could possibly have. The glass windows made the inside of that house so light that you would hardly know you were in a house. It smelled clean and piny, from the yellow-new board walls and floor. The cookstove stood lordly in the corner by the lean-to door. A touch on the the white-china door knob swung the bought door on its bought hinges, and the door knob's little iron tongue clicked and held the door shut.

'We'll move in, tomorrow morning,' Pa said. 'This is the last night we'll sleep in a dugout.'

Laura and Mary took his hands and they went down the knoll. The wheat-field was a silky, shimmery green rippling over a curve of the prairie. Its sides were straight and its corners square, and all around it the prairie grasses looked coarser and darker green. Laura looked back at the wonderful house. In the sunshine on the knoll, its sawed-lumber walls and roof were as golden as a straw-stack.

17
Moving In

In the sunny morning Ma and Laura helped carry everything from the dugout up to the top of the bank and load it in the wagon. Laura hardly dared look at Pa; they were bursting with the secret surprise for Ma.

Ma did not suspect anything. She took the hot ashes out of the little old stove so that Pa could handle it. She asked Pa, 'Did you remember to get more stovepipe?'

'Yes, Caroline,' Pa said. Laura did not laugh, but she choked.

'Goodness, Laura,' Ma said, 'have you got a frog in your throat?'

David and Sam hauled the wagon away, across the ford and back over the prairie, up to the new house. Ma and Mary and Laura, with armfuls of things, and Carrie toddling ahead, went over the footbridge and up the grassy path. The sawed-lumber house with its bought-shingle roof was all golden on the knoll, and Pa jumped off the wagon and waited to be with Ma when she saw the cookstove.

She walked into the house and stopped short. Her

mouth opened and shut. Then she said, weakly, 'My land!'

Laura and Mary whooped and danced, and so did Carrie, though she did not know why.

'It's yours, Ma! It's your new cookstove!' they shouted. 'It's got an oven! And four lids, and a little handle!'

Mary said. 'It's got letters on it and I can read them! PAT, Pat!'

'Oh, Charles, you shouldn't!' Ma said.

Pa hugged her. 'Don't you worry, Caroline!' he told her.

'I never have worried, Charles,' Ma answered. 'But building such a house, and glass windows, and buying a stove – it's too much.'

'Nothing's too much for you,' said Pa. 'And don't worry about the expense. Just look through that glass at that wheat-field!'

But Laura and Mary pulled her to the cookstove. She lifted the lids as Laura showed her, she watched while Mary worked the draught, she looked at the oven.

'My!' she said. 'I don't know if I dare try to get dinner on such a big, beautiful stove!'

But she did get dinner on that wonderful stove and Mary and Laura set the table in the bright, airy room. The glass windows were open, air and light came in from every side, and sunshine was streaming in through the doorway and the shining window beside it.

It was such fun to eat in that big, airy, light house that after dinner they sat at the table, just enjoying being there.

'Now this is something like!' Pa said.

Then they put up the curtains. Glass windows must have curtains, and Ma had made them of pieces of worn-out sheets, starched crisp and white as snow. She had edged them with narrow strips of pretty calico. The curtains in the big room were edged with pink strips from Carrie's little dress that had been torn when the oxen ran away. The bedroom curtains were edged with strips from Mary's old blue dress. That was the pink calico and the blue calico that Pa brought home from town, long ago in the Big Woods.

While Pa was driving nails to hold the strings for the curtains, Ma brought out two long strips of brown wrapping-paper that she had saved. She folded them, and she showed Mary and Laura how to cut tiny bits out of the folded paper with the scissors. When each unfolded her paper, there was a row of stars.

Ma spread the paper on the shelves behind the stove. The stars hung over the edges of the shelves, and the light shone through them.

When the curtains were up, Ma hung two snowy-clean sheets across a corner of the bedroom. That made a nice place where Pa and Ma could hang their clothes. Up in the attic, Ma put up another sheet that Mary and Laura could hang their clothes behind.

The house was beautiful when Ma had finished. The pure-white curtains were looped back on each side of the clear glass windows. Between those pink-edged, snowy curtains the sunshine streamed in. The walls were all clean, piny-smelling boards, with the skeleton of the house against them, and the ladder going up to the attic. The cookstove and its stovepipe were glossy black, and in that corner were the starry shelves.

Ma spread the between-meals red-checked cloth on the table, and on it she set the shining-clean lamp. She laid there the paper-covered Bible, the big green *Wonders of the Animal World,* and the novel named *Millbank.* The two benches stood neatly by the table.

The last thing, Pa hung the bracket on the wall by the front window, and Ma stood the little china shepherdess on it.

That was the wood-brown bracket that Pa had carved with stars and vines and flowers, for Ma's Christmas long ago. That was the same smiling little shepherdess, with golden hair and blue eyes and pink cheeks, her little china bodice laced with china-gold ribbons and her little china apron and her little china shoes. She had travelled from the Big Woods all the way to Indian Territory, and all the way to Plum Creek in Minnesota, and there she stood smiling. She was not broken. She was not nicked nor even scratched. She was the same little shepherdess, smiling the same smile.

That night Mary and Laura climbed the ladder and went to bed by themselves in their large, airy, very own attic. They did not have curtains because Ma had no more old sheets. But each had a box to sit on, and each had a box to keep her treasures in. Charlotte and the paper dolls lived in Laura's box, and Mary's quilt blocks and her scrapbag were in Mary's box. Behind the curtain each had her nail, to take her nightgown off and hang her dress on. The single thing wrong with that room was that Jack could not climb up the ladder.

Laura went to sleep at once. She had been running in and out of the new house and up and down the ladder all day long. But she could not stay asleep. The new house was so still. She missed the sound of the creek singing to her in her sleep. The stillness kept waking her.

At last it was a sound that opened her eyes. She listened. It was a sound of many, many little feet running about overhead. It seemed to be thousands of little animals scampering on the roof. What could it be?

Why, it was raindrops! Laura had not heard rain pattering on the roof for so long that she had forgotten the sound of it. In the dugout she could not hear rain, there was so much earth and grass above her.

She was happy while she lay drowsing to sleep again, hearing the pitter-pat-patter of rain on the roof.

18
The Old Crab and the Bloodsuckers

When Laura jumped out of bed in the morning, her bare feet landed on a smooth, wooden floor. She smelled the piny smell of boards. Overhead was the slanting roof of yellow-bright shingles and the rafters holding them up.

From the eastern window she saw the little path going down the grassy knoll. She saw a square corner of the pale-green, silky wheat-field, and beyond it the grey-green oats. Far, far away was the edge of the great, green earth, and a silver streak of the sun's edge peeping over it. The willow creek and the dugout seemed far away and long ago.

Suddenly, warm yellow sunshine poured over her in her nightgown. On the clean wood-yellow floor the panes of the window were sunshine, the little bars between them were shadow, and Laura's head in the nightcap, her braids, and her hands with all the separate fingers when she held them up, were darker, solid shadow.

Downstairs the lids clattered on the new, fine cookstove. Ma's voice came up through the square hole where the

106

ladder went down. 'Mary! Laura! Time to get up, girls!'

That was the way a new day began in the new house.

But while they were eating breakfast in the large, airy downstairs Laura wanted to see the creek. She asked Pa if she might go back to play there.

'No, Laura,' Pa said. 'I don't want you to go back to that creek, where the dark, deep holes are. But when your work is done, you and Mary run along that path that Nelson made coming to work, and see what you find!'

They hurried to do the work. And in the lean-to they found a bought broom! There seemed no end to the wonders in this house. This broom had a long, straight, perfectly round, smooth handle. The broom part was made of thousands of thin, stiff, greeny-yellow bristles. Ma said they were broom straws. They were cut absolutely straight across the bottom, and they curved at the top into fiat, firm shoulders. Stitches of red string held them tight. This broom was nothing like the round, willow-bough brooms that Pa made. It seemed too fine to sweep with. And it glided over the smooth floor like magic.

Still, Laura and Mary could hardly wait to follow that path. They worked fast; they put away the broom, and they started. Laura was in such a hurry that she walked nicely only a few steps, then she began to run. Her bonnet slid back and hung by its strings around her neck and her bare feet flew over the dim, grassy path, down the knoll, across a bit of level land, up a low slope. And there was the creek!

Laura was astonished. This was such a different-looking creek, too, so gentle in the sun between its low, grassy banks.

The path stopped in the shade of a great willow tree. A footbridge went on across the water to level, sunny grass. Then the dim path wandered on until it curved around a tiny hill and went out of sight.

Laura thought that little path went on for ever wandering on sunny grass and crossing friendly streams and always going around low hills to see what was on the other side. She knew it really must go to Mr Nelson's house, but it was a little path that did not want to stop anywhere. It wanted always to be going on.

The creek came flowing out of a thicket of plum trees. The low trees grew thickly on both sides of the narrow water, and their boughs almost touched above it. The water was dark in their shade.

Then it spread out and ran wide and shallow, dimpling and splashing over sand and gravel. It narrowed to slide under the footbridge and ran on gurgling till it stopped in a large pool. The pool was glassy-still by a clump of willows.

Laura waited till Mary came. Then they went wading in the shallow water over the sparkling sand and pebbles. Tiny minnows swam in swarms around their toes. When they stood still the minnows nibbled at their feet. Suddenly Laura saw a strange creature in the water.

He was almost as long as Laura's foot. He was sleek and greeny-brown. In front he had two long arms that ended in big, flat, pincer-claws. Along his sides were short legs, and his strong tail was flat and scaly, with a thin forked fin at the end. Bristles stuck out of his nose, and his eyes were round and bulging.

'What's that!' Mary said. She was scared.

Laura did not go any nearer him. She bent down cautiously to see him, and suddenly he was not there. Faster than a water-bug, he shot backward, and a little curl of muddy water came out from under a flat rock where he had gone.

In a minute he thrust out a claw and snapped it. Then he looked out.

When Laura waded nearer, he flipped backwards under the stone. But when she splashed water at his stone, he ran out, snapping his claws, trying to catch her bare toes. Then Laura and Mary ran screaming and splashing away from his home.

They teased him with a long stick. His big claw snapped

that stick right in two. They got a bigger stick, and he clamped his claw and did not let go till Laura lifted him out of the water. His eyes glared and his tail curled under him, and his other claw was snapping. Then he let go and dropped, and flipped under his stone again.

He always came out, fighting mad, when they splashed at his stone. And they always ran screaming away from his frightful claws.

They sat for a while on the footbridge in the shade of the big willow. They listened to the water running and watched its sparkles. Then they went wading again, all the way to the plum thicket.

Mary would not go into the dark water under the plum trees. The creek bottom was muddy there and she did not like to wade in mud. So she sat on the bank while Laura waded into the thicket.

The water was still there, with old leaves floating on its edges. The mud squelched between Laura's toes and came up in clouds till she could not see the bottom. The air smelled old and musty. So Laura turned around and waded back into the clean water and the sunshine.

There seemed to be some blobs of mud on her legs and feet. She splashed the clear water over them to wash them off. But they did not wash off. Her hand could not scrape them off.

They were the colour of mud, they were soft like mud. But they stuck as tight as Laura's skin.

Laura screamed. She stood there screaming, 'Oh, Mary, Mary! Come! Quick!'

Mary came, but she would not touch those horrible things. She said they were worms. Worms made her sick. Laura felt sicker than Mary, but it was more awful to have those things on her than it was to touch them. She took hold of one, she dug her fingernails into it, and pulled.

The thing stretched out long, and longer, and longer, and still it hung on.

'Oh don't! Oh don't! Oh, you'll pull it in two!' Mary said. But Laura pulled it out longer, till it came off. Blood trickled down her leg from the place where it had been.

One by one, Laura pulled those things off. A little trickle of blood ran down where each one let go.

Laura did not feel like playing any more. She washed her hands and her legs in the clean water and she went to the house with Mary.

It was dinner-time and Pa was there. Laura told him about those mud-brown things without eyes or head or legs, that had fastened to her skin in the creek.

Ma said they were leeches and that doctors put them on sick people. But Pa called them bloodsuckers. He said they lived in the mud, in dark, still places in the water.

'I don't like them,' Laura said.

'Then stay out of the mud, flutterbudget,' said Pa. 'If you don't want trouble, don't go looking for it.'

Ma said, 'Well, you girls won't have much time for playing in the creek, anyway. Now we're nicely settled and only two and a half miles from town, you can go to school.'

Laura could not say a word. Neither could Mary. They looked at each other and thought, 'School?'

19

The Fish-Trap

The more Laura was told about school, the more she did not want to go there. She did not know how she could stay away from the creek all day long. She asked, 'Oh, Ma, do I have to?'

Ma said that a great girl almost eight years old should be learning to read instead of running wild on the banks of Plum Creek.

'But I can read, Ma,' Laura begged. 'Please don't make me go to school. I can read. Listen!'

She took the book named *Millbank*, and opened it, and looking up anxiously at Ma she read, 'The doors and windows of Millbank were closed. Crape streamed from the door knob –'

'Oh, Laura,' Ma said, 'you are not reading! You are only reciting what you've heard me read to Pa so often. Besides, there are other things to learn – spelling and writing and arithmetic. Don't say any more about it. You will start to school with Mary Monday morning.'

Mary was sitting down to sew. She looked like a good little girl who wanted to go to school.

Just outside the lean-to door Pa was hammering at something. Laura went bounding out so quickly that his hammer nearly hit her.

'Oop!' said Pa. 'Nearly hit you that time. I should have expected you, flutterbudget. You're always on hand like a sore thumb.'

'Oh, what are you doing, Pa?' Laura asked him. He was nailing together some narrow strips of board left from the house-building.

'Making a fish-trap,' said Pa. 'Want to help me? You can hand me the nails.'

One by one, Laura handed him the nails, and Pa drove them in. They were making a skeleton box. It was a long, narrow box without a top, and Pa left wide cracks between the strips of wood.

'How will that catch fish?' Laura asked. 'If you put it in the creek they will swim in through the cracks but they will swim right out again.'

'You wait and see,' said Pa.

Laura waited till Pa put away the nails and hammer. He put the fish-trap on his shoulder and said, 'You can come help me set it.'

Laura took his hand and skipped beside him down the knoll and across the level land to the creek. They went along the low bank, past the plum thicket. The banks were steeper here, the creek was narrower, and its noise was louder. Pa went crashing down through bushes, Laura climbed scrooging down under them, and there was a waterfall.

The water ran swift and smooth to the edge and fell over it with a loud, surprised crash-splashing. From the bottom it rushed up again and whirled around, then it jumped and hurried away.

Laura would never have tired of watching it. But she must help Pa set the fish-trap. They put it exactly under the waterfall. The whole waterfall went into the trap, and boiled up again more surprised than before. It could not jump out of the trap. It foamed out through the cracks.

'Now you see, Laura,' said Pa. 'The fish will come over the falls into the trap, and the little ones will go out through the cracks, but the big ones can't. They can't climb back up the falls. So they'll have to stay swimming in the box till I come and take them out.'

At that very minute a big fish came slithering over the falls. Laura squealed and shouted, 'Look, Pa! Look!'

Pa's hands in the water grabbed the fish and lifted him out, flopping. Laura almost fell into the waterfall. They looked at that silvery fat fish and then Pa dropped him into the trap again.

'Oh Pa, can't we please stay and catch enough fish for supper?' Laura asked.

'I've got to get to work on a sod barn, Laura,' said Pa. 'And plough the garden and dig a well and –' Then he looked at Laura and said, 'Well, little half-pint, maybe it won't take long.'

He sat on his heels and Laura sat on hers and they

waited. The creek poured and splashed, always the same and always changing. Glints of sunshine danced on it. Cool air came up from it and warm air lay on Laura's neck. The bushes held up thousands of little leaves against the sky. They smelled warm and sweet in the sun.

'Oh, Pa,' Laura said, 'do I have to go to school?'

'You will like school, Laura,' said Pa.

'I like it better here,' Laura said, mournfully.

'I know, little half-pint,' said Pa, 'but it isn't everybody that gets a chance to learn to read and write and cipher. Your Ma was a school-teacher when we met, and when she came West with me I promised that our girls would have a chance to get book learning. That's why we stopped here, so close to a town that has a school. You're almost eight years old now, and Mary going on nine, and it's time you began. Be thankful you've got the chance, Laura.'

'Yes, Pa,' Laura sighed. Just then another big fish came over the falls. Before Pa could catch it, here came another!

Pa cut and peeled a forked stick. He took four big fish out of the trap and strung them on the stick. Laura and Pa went back to the house, carrying those flopping fish. Ma's eyes were round when she saw them. Pa cut off their heads and stripped out their insides and showed Laura how to scale fish. He scaled three, and she scaled almost all of one. Ma rolled them in meal and fried them in fat, and they all ate good fish for supper.

'You always think of something, Charles,' said Ma. 'Just when I'm wondering where our living is to come from, now it's spring.' Pa could not hunt in the springtime, for then all the rabbits had little rabbits and the birds had little birds in their nests.

'Wait till I harvest that wheat!' Pa said. 'Then we'll have salt pork every day. Yes, by gravy, and fresh beef!'

Every morning after that, before he went to work, Pa brought fish from the trap. He never took more than they needed to eat. The others he lifted out of the trap and let swim away.

He brought buffalo fish and pickerel, and catfish, and shiners, and bullheads with two black horns. He brought some whose names he did not know. Every day there was fish for breakfast and fish for dinner and fish for supper.

20

School

Monday morning came. As soon as Laura and Mary had washed the breakfast dishes, they went up the ladder and put on their Sunday dresses. Mary's was a blue-sprigged calico, and Laura's was red-sprigged.

Ma braided their hair very tightly and bound the ends with thread. They could not wear their Sunday hair-ribbons because they might lose them. They put on their sunbonnets, freshly washed and ironed.

Then Ma took them into the bedroom. She knelt down by the box where she kept her best things, and she took out three books. They were the books she had studied when she was a little girl. One was a speller, and one was a reader, and one was a 'rithmetic.

She looked solemnly at Mary and Laura, and they were solemn, too.

'I am giving you these books for your very own, Mary and Laura,' Ma said. 'I know you will take care of them and study them faithfully.'

'Yes, Ma,' they said.

She gave Mary the books to carry. She gave Laura the

little tin pail with their lunch in it, under a clean cloth.

'Goodbye,' she said. 'Be good girls.'

Ma and Carrie stood in the doorway, and Jack went with them down the knoll. He was puzzled. They went on across the grass where the tracks of Pa's wagon wheels went, and Jack stayed close beside Laura.

When they came to the ford of the creek, he sat down and whined anxiously. Laura had to explain to him that he must not come any farther. She stroked his big head and tried to smooth out the worried wrinkles. But he sat watching and frowning while they waded across the shallow, wide ford.

They waded carefully and did not splash their clean dresses. A blue heron rose from the water, flapping away with his long legs dangling. Laura and Mary stepped carefully on to the grass. They would not walk in the dusty wheel tracks until their feet were dry, because their feet must be clean when they came to town.

The new house looked small on its knoll with the great green prairie spreading far around it. Ma and Carrie had gone inside. Only Jack sat watching by the ford.

Mary and Laura walked on quietly.

Dew was sparkling on the grass. Meadow larks were singing. Snipes were walking on their long, thin legs. Prairie hens were clucking and tiny prairie chicks were peeping. Rabbits stood up with paws dangling, long ears twitching, and their round eyes staring at Mary and Laura.

Pa had said that town was only two and a half miles away, and the road would take them to it. They would know they were in town when they came to a house.

Large white clouds sailed in the enormous sky and their grey shadows trailed across the waving prairie grasses. The road always ended a little way ahead, but when they came to that ending, the road was going on. It was only the tracks of Pa's wagon through the grass.

'For pity's sake, Laura,' said Mary, 'keep your sunbonnet on! You'll be brown as an Indian, and what will the town girls think of us?'

'I don't care!' said Laura, loudly and bravely.

'You do, too!' said Mary.

'I don't either!' said Laura.

'You do!'

'I don't!'

'You're just as scared of town as I am,' said Mary.

Laura did not answer. After a while she took hold of her sunbonnet strings and pulled the bonnet up over her head.

'Anyway, there's two of us,' Mary said.

They went on and on. After a long time they saw town. It looked like small blocks of wood on the prairie. When the road dipped down, they saw only grasses again and the sky. Then they saw the town again, always larger. Smoke went up from its stovepipes.

The clean, grassy road ended in dust. This dusty road went by a small house and then past a store. The store had a porch with steps going up to it.

Beyond the store there was a blacksmith shop. It stood back from the road, with a bare place in front of it. Inside it a big man in a leather apron made a bellows puff! puff! at red coals. He took a white-hot iron out of the coals with tongs, and swung a big hammer down on it, whang! Dozens of sparks flew out tiny in the daylight.

Beyond the bare place was the back of a building. Mary and Laura walked close to the side of this building. The ground was hard there. There was no more grass to walk on.

In front of this building, another wide, dusty road crossed their road. Mary and Laura stopped. They looked across the dust at the fronts of two more stores. They heard a confused noise of children's voices. Pa's road did not go any farther.

'Come on,' said Mary, low. But she stood still. 'It's the school where we hear the hollering. Pa said we would hear it.'

Laura wanted to turn around and run all the way home.

She and Mary went slowly walking out into the dust and turned towards that noise of voices. They went padding along between two stores. They passed piles of boards and shingles; that must be the lumber-yard where Pa got the boards for the new house. Then they saw the schoolhouse.

It was out on the prairie beyond the end of the dusty road. A long path went towards it through the grass. Boys and girls were in front of it.

Laura went along the path towards them and Mary came behind her. All those girls and boys stopped their noise and looked. Laura kept on going nearer and nearer all those eyes, and suddenly, without meaning to, she swung the dinner-pail and called out, 'You all sounded just like a flock of prairie chickens!'

They were surprised. But they were not as much surprised as Laura. She was ashamed, too. Mary gasped, 'Laura!' Then a freckled boy with fire-coloured hair yelled, 'Snipes, yourselves! Snipes! Snipes! Long-legged snipes!'

Laura wanted to sink down and hide her legs. Her dress was too short, it was much shorter than the town girls' dresses. So was Mary's. Before they came to Plum Creek, Ma had said they were outgrowing those dresses. Their bare legs did look long and spindly, like snipes' legs.

All the boys were pointing and yelling, 'Snipes! Snipes!'

Then a red-headed girl began pushing those boys and saying: 'Shut up! You make too much noise! Shut up, Sandy!' she said to the red-headed boy, and he shut up. She came close to Laura and said:

'My name is Christy Kennedy, and that horrid boy is my brother Sandy, but he doesn't mean any harm. What's your name?'

Her red hair was braided so tightly that the braids were stiff. Her eyes were dark blue, almost black, and her round cheeks were freckled. Her sunbonnet hung down her back.

'Is that your sister?' she said. 'Those are my sisters.' Some big girls were talking to Mary. 'The big one's Nettie, and the black-haired one's Cassie, and then there's

Donald and me and Sandy. How many brothers and sisters have you?'

'Two,' Laura said. 'That's Mary, and Carrie's the baby. She has golden hair, too. And we have a bulldog named Jack. We live on Plum Creek. Where do you live?'

'Does your Pa drive two bay horses with black manes and tails?' Christy asked.

'Yes,' said Laura. 'They are Sam and David, our Christmas horses.'

'He comes by our house, so you came by it, too,' said Christy. 'It's the house before you came to Beadle's store and post-office, before you get to the blacksmith shop. Miss Eva Beadle's our teacher. That's Nellie Oleson.'

Nellie Oleson was very pretty. Her yellow hair hung in long curls, with two big blue ribbon bows on top. Her dress was thin white lawn, with little blue flowers scattered over it, and she wore shoes.

She looked at Laura and she looked at Mary, and she wrinkled up her nose.

'Hm!' she said. 'Country girls!'

Before anyone else could say anything, a bell rang. A young lady stood in the schoolhouse doorway, swinging the bell in her hand. All the boys and girls hurried by her into the schoolhouse.

She was a beautiful young lady. Her brown hair was

frizzed in bangs over her brown eyes, and done in thick braids behind. Buttons sparkled all down the front of her bodice, and her skirts were drawn back tightly and fell down behind in big puffs and loops. Her face was sweet and her smile was lovely.

She laid her hand on Laura's shoulder and said, 'You're a new little girl, aren't you?'

'Yes, ma'am,' said Laura.

'And is this your sister?' Teacher asked, smiling at Mary.

'Yes, ma'am,' said Mary.

Then come with me,' said Teacher, 'and I'll write your names in my book.'

They went with her the whole length of the schoolhouse, and stepped up on the platform.

The schoolhouse was a room made of new boards. Its ceiling was the underneath of shingles, like the attic ceiling. Long benches stood one behind another down the middle of the room. They were made of planed boards. Each bench had a back, and two shelves stuck out from the back, over the bench behind. Only the front bench did not have any shelves in front of it, and the last bench did not have any back.

There were two glass windows in each side of the schoolhouse. They were open, and so was the door. The wind came in, and the sound of waving grasses, and the smell and the sight of the endless prairie and the great light of the sky.

Laura saw all this while she stood with Mary by Teacher's desk and they told her their names and how old they were. She did not move her head, but her eyes looked around.

A water-pail stood on a bench by the door. A bought broom stood in one corner. On the wall behind Teacher's desk there was a smooth space of boards painted black. Under it was a little trough. Some kind of short, white sticks lay in the trough, and a block of wood with a woolly bit of sheepskin pulled tightly around it and nailed down. Laura wondered what those things were.

Mary showed Teacher how much she could read and spell. But Laura looked at Ma's book and shook her head. She could not read. She was not even sure of all the letters.

'Well, you can begin at the beginning, Laura,' said Teacher, 'and Mary can study farther on. Have you a slate?'

They did not have a slate.

'I will lend you mine,' Teacher said. 'You cannot learn to write without a slate.'

She lifted up the top of her desk and took out the slate. The desk was made like a tall box, with one side cut out for her knees. The top rose up on bought hinges, and under it was the place where she kept things. Her books were there, and the ruler.

Laura did not know until later that the ruler was to punish anyone who fidgeted or whispered in school. Anyone who was so naughty had to walk up to Teacher's desk and hold out her hand while Teacher slapped it many times, hard, with the ruler.

But Laura and Mary never whispered in school, and they always tried not to fidget. They sat side by side on a bench and studied. Mary's feet rested on the floor, but Laura's dangled. They held their book open on the board shelf before them, Laura studying at the front of the book and Mary studying farther on, and the pages between standing straight up.

Laura was a whole class by herself, because she was the only pupil who could not read. Whenever Teacher had time, she called Laura to her desk and helped her read letters. Just before dinner-time that first day, Laura was able to read, C A T, cat. Suddenly she remembered and said, 'P A T, Pat!'

Teacher was surprised.

'R A T, rat!' said Teacher. 'M A T, mat!' And Laura was reading! She could read the whole first row in the speller.

At noon all the other children and Teacher went home to dinner. Laura and Mary took their dinner-pail and sat in the grass against the shady side of the empty schoolhouse. They ate their bread and butter and talked.

'I like school,' Mary said.

'So do I,' said Laura. 'Only it makes my legs tired. But I don't like that Nellie Oleson that called us country girls.'

'We are country girls,' said Mary.

'Yes, and she needn't wrinkle her nose!' Laura said.

21

Nellie Oleson

Jack was waiting to meet them at the ford that night, and at supper they told Pa and Ma all about school. When they said they were using Teacher's slate, Pa shook his head. They must not be beholden for the loan of a slate.

Next morning he took his money out of the fiddle-box and counted it. He gave Mary a round silver piece to buy a slate.

'There's plenty of fish in the creek,' he said. 'We'll hold out till wheat-harvest.'

'There'll be potatoes pretty soon, too,' said Ma. She tied the money in a handkerchief and pinned it inside Mary's pocket.

Mary clutched that pocket all the way along the prairie road. The wind was blowing. Butterflies and birds were flying over the waving grasses and wild flowers. The rabbits loped before the wind and the great clear sky curved over it all. Laura swung the dinner-pail and hippety-hopped.

In town, they crossed dusty Main Street and climbed

the steps to Mr Oleson's store. Pa had said to buy the slate there.

Inside the store there was a long board counter. The wall behind it was covered with shelves, full of tin pans and pots and lamps and lanterns and bolts of coloured cloth. By the other wall stood ploughs and kegs of nails and rolls of wire, and on that wall hung saws and hammers and hatchets and knives.

A large, round, yellow cheese was on the counter, and on the floor in front of it was a barrel of molasses, and a whole keg of pickles, and a big wooden box full of crackers, and two tall wooden pails of candy. It was Christmas candy; two big pails full of it.

Suddenly the back door of the store burst open, and Nellie Oleson and her little brother Willie came bouncing in. Nellie's nose wrinkled at Laura and Mary, and Willie yahed at them: 'Yah! Yah! Long-legged snipes!'

'Shut up, Willie,' Mr Oleson said. But Willie did not shut up. He went on saying: 'Snipes! Snipes!'

Nellie flounced by Mary and Laura, and dug her hands into a pail of candy. Willie dug into the other pail. They grabbed all the candy they could hold and stood cramming it into their mouths. They stood in front of Mary and Laura, looking at them, and did not offer them even one piece.

'Nellie! You and Willie go right back out of here!' Mr Oleson said.

They went on stuffing candy into their mouths and staring at Mary and Laura. Mr Oleson took no more notice of them. Mary gave him the money and he gave her the slate. He said: 'You'll want a slate pencil, too. Here it is. One penny.'

Nellie said, 'They haven't got a penny.'

'Well, take it along, and tell your Pa to give me the penny next time he comes to town,' said Mr Oleson.

'No, sir. Thank you,' Mary said. She turned around and so did Laura, and they walked out of the store. At the door Laura looked back. And Nellie made a face at her. Nellie's tongue was streaked red and green from the candy.

'My goodness!' Mary said. 'I couldn't be as mean as that Nellie Oleson.'

Laura thought: 'I could. I could be meaner to her than she is to us, if Ma and Pa would let me.'

They looked at their slate's smooth, soft-grey surface, and its clean, flat wooden frame, cunningly fitted together at the corners. It was a handsome slate. But they must have a slate pencil.

Pa had already spent so much for the slate that they hated to tell him they must have another penny. They walked along soberly, till suddenly Laura remembered their Christmas pennies. They still had those pennies that they had found in their stockings on Christmas morning in Indian Territory.

Mary had a penny, and Laura had a penny, but they needed only one slate pencil. So they decided that Mary would spend her penny for the pencil and after that she would own half of Laura's penny. Next morning they bought the pencil, but they did not buy it from Mr Oleson. They bought it at Mr Beadle's store and post-office, where Teacher lived, and that morning they walked on to school with Teacher.

All through the long, hot weeks they went to school, and every day they liked it more. They liked reading, writing, and arithmetic. They liked spelling-down on Friday afternoons. And Laura loved recess, when the little girls rushed out into the sun and wind, picking wild flowers among the prairie grasses and playing games.

The boys played boys' games on one side of the schoolhouse; the little girls played on the other side, and Mary sat with the other big girls, ladylike on the steps.

The little girls always played ring-around-a-rosy, because Nellie Oleson said to. They got tired of it, but they always played it, till one day, before Nellie could say anything, Laura said, 'Let's play Uncle John!'

'Let's! Let's!' the girls said, taking hold of hands. But

Nellie grabbed both hands full of Laura's long hair and jerked her flat on the ground.

'No! No!' Nellie shouted. 'I want to play ring-around-a-rosy!'

Laura jumped up and her hand flashed out to slap Nellie. She stopped it just in time. Pa said she must never strike anybody.

'Come on, Laura,' Christy said, taking her hands. Laura's face felt bursting and she could hardly see, but she went circling with the others around Nellie. Nellie tossed her curls and flounced her skirts because she had her way. Then Christy began singing and all the others joined in:

> 'Uncle John is sick abed.
> What shall we send him?'

'No! No! Ring-around-a-rosy!' Nellie screamed. 'Or I won't play!' She broke through the ring and no one went after her.

'All right, you get in the middle, Maud,' Christy said, They began again.

> 'Uncle John is sick abed.
> What shall we send him?
> A piece of pie, a piece of cake,

Apple and dumpling!
What shall we send it in?
A golden saucer.
Who shall we send it by?
The governor's daughter.
If the governor's daughter ain't at home,
Who shall we send it by?'

Then all the girls shouted,

'By Laura Ingalls!'

Laura stepped into the middle of the ring and they danced around her. They went on playing Uncle John till Teacher rang the bell. Nellie was in the schoolhouse, crying, and she said she was so mad that she was never going to speak to Laura or Christy again.

But the next week she asked all the girls to a party at her house on Saturday afternoon. She asked Christy and Laura, specially.

22

Town Party

Laura and Mary had never been to a party and did not quite know what it would be like. Ma said it was a pleasant time that friends had together.

After school on Friday she washed their dresses and sunbonnets. Saturday morning she ironed them, fresh and crisp. Laura and Mary bathed that morning, too, instead of that night.

'You look sweet and pretty as posies,' Ma said when they came down the ladder, dressed for the party. She tied on their hair-ribbons and warned them not to lose them. 'Now be good girls,' she said, 'and mind your manners.'

When they came to town they stopped for Cassie and Christy. Cassie and Christy had never been to a party, either. They all went timidly into Mr Oleson's store, and Mr Oleson told them, 'Go right on in!'

So they went past the candy and pickles and ploughs, to the back door of the store. It opened, and there stood Nellie all dressed up, and Mrs Oleson asking them in.

Laura had never seen such a fine room. She could hardly

say 'Good afternoon, Mrs Oleson,' and 'Yes, ma'am,' and 'No, ma'am.'

The whole floor was covered with some kind of heavy cloth that felt rough under Laura's bare feet. It was brown and green, with red and yellow scrolls all over it. The walls and the ceiling were narrow, smooth boards fitted together with a crease between them. The table and chairs were of a yellow wood that shone like glass, and their legs were perfectly round. There were coloured pictures on the walls.

'Go into the bedroom, girls, and leave your bonnets,' Mrs Oleson said in a company voice.

The bedstead was shiny wood, too. There were two other pieces of furniture. One was made of drawers on top of each other, with two little drawers sitting on its top, and two curved pieces of wood went up and held a big looking-glass between them. On top of the other stood a china pitcher in a big china bowl, and a small china dish with a piece of soap on it.

There were glass windows in both rooms, and the curtains of those windows were white lace.

Behind the front room was a big lean-to with a cook-stove in it, like Ma's new one, and all kinds of tin pots and pans hanging on the walls.

All the girls were there now, and Mrs Oleson's skirts

went rustling among them. Laura wanted to be still and look at things, but Mrs Oleson said, 'Now, Nellie, bring out your playthings.'

'They can play with Willie's playthings,' Nellie said.

'They can't ride on my velocipede!' Willie shouted.

'Well, they can play with your Noah's ark and your soldiers,' said Nellie, and Mrs Oleson made Willie be quiet.

The Noah's ark was the most wonderful thing that Laura had ever seen. They all knelt down and squealed and shouted and laughed over it. There were zebras and elephants and tigers and horses; all kinds of animals, just as if the picture had come out of the paper-covered Bible at home.

And there were two whole armies of tin soldiers, with uniforms painted bright blue and bright red.

There was a jumping-jack. He was cut out of thin, flat wood; striped paper trousers and jacket were pasted on him, and his face was painted white with red cheeks and circles around his eyes, and his tall cap was pointed. He hung between two thin red strips of wood, and when you squeezed them he danced. His hands held on to twisted strings. He would turn a somersault over the strings; he would stand on his head with his toe on his nose.

Even the big girls were chattering and squealing over

those animals and those soldiers, and they laughed at the jumping-jack till they cried.

Then Nellie walked among them, saying, 'You can look at my doll.'

The doll had a china head, with smooth red cheeks and red mouth. Her eyes were black and her china hair was black and waved. Her wee hands were china, and her feet were tiny china feet in black china shoes.

'Oh!' Laura said. 'Oh, what a beautiful doll! Oh, Nellie, what is her name?'

'She's nothing but an old doll,' Nellie said. 'I don't care about this old doll. You wait till you see my wax doll.'

She threw the china doll in a drawer, and she took out a long box. She put the box on the bed and took off its lid. All the girls leaned around her to look.

There lay a doll that seemed to be alive. Real golden hair lay in soft curls on her little pillow. Her lips were parted, showing two tiny white teeth. Her eyes were closed. The doll was sleeping there in the box.

Nellie lifted her up, and her eyes opened wide. They were big blue eyes. She seemed to laugh. Her arms stretched out and she said, 'Mamma!'

'She does that when I squeeze her stomach,' Nellie said. 'Look!' She punched the doll's stomach hard with her fist, and the poor doll cried out, 'Mamma!'

She was dressed in blue silk. Her petticoats were real petticoats trimmed with ruffles and lace, and her panties were real little panties that would come off. On her feet were real little blue leather slippers.

All this time Laura had not said a word. She couldn't.

She did not think of actually touching that marvellous doll, but without meaning to, her finger reached out towards the blue silk.

'Don't you touch her!' Nellie screeched. 'You keep your hands off my doll, Laura Ingalls!'

She snatched the doll against her and turned her back so Laura could not see her putting her back in the box.

Laura's face burned hot and the other girls did not know what to do. Laura went and sat on a chair. The others watched Nellie put the box in a drawer and shut it. Then they looked at the animals and the soldiers again and squeezed the jumping-jack.

Mrs Oleson came in and asked Laura why she was not playing. Laura said, 'I would rather sit here, thank you, ma'am.'

'Would you like to look at these?' Mrs Oleson asked her, and she laid two books in Laura's lap.

'Thank you, ma'am,' Laura said.

She turned the pages of the books carefully. One was not exactly a book; it was thin and it had no covers. It was a little magazine, all for children. The other was a book with a thick, glossy cover, and on the cover was a picture of an old woman wearing a peaked cap and riding on a broom across a huge yellow moon. Over her head large letters said, MOTHER GOOSE.

Laura had not known there were such wonderful books in the world. On every page of that book there was a picture and a rhyme. Laura could read some of them. She forgot all about the party.

Suddenly Mrs Oleson was saying: 'Come, little girl. You mustn't let the others eat all the cake, must you?'

'Yes, ma'am,' Laura said. 'No, ma'am.'

A glossy white cloth covered the table. On it was a beautiful sugar-white cake and tall glasses.

'I got the biggest piece!' Nellie shouted, grabbing a big piece out of that cake. The others sat waiting till Mrs Oleson gave them their pieces. She put each piece on a china plate.

'Is your lemonade sweet enough?' Mrs Oleson asked. So Laura knew that it was lemonade in the glasses. She had never tasted anything like it. At first it was sweet, but after she ate a bit of the sugar-white off her piece of cake, the lemonade was sour. But they all answered Mrs Oleson politely, 'Yes, thank you, ma'am.'

They were careful not to let a crumb of cake fall on the tablecloth. They did not spill one drop of lemonade.

Then it was time to go home, and Laura remembered to say, as Ma had told them to: 'Thank you, Mrs Oleson. I had a very good time at the party.' So did all the others.

When they were out of the store, Christy said to Laura, 'I wish you'd slapped that mean Nellie Oleson.'

'Oh no! I couldn't!' Laura said. 'But I'm going to get even with her. Sh! Don't let Mary know I said that.'

Jack was waiting lonesome at the ford. It was Saturday, and Laura had not played with him. It would be a whole week before they would have another day of playing along Plum Creek.

They told Ma all about the party, and she said, 'We must not accept hospitality without making some return. I've been thinking about it, girls, and you must ask Nellie Oleson and the others to a party here. I think a week from Saturday.'

23

Country Party

'Will you come to my party?' Laura asked Christy and Maud and Nellie Oleson. Mary asked the big girls. They all said they would come.

That Saturday morning the new house was specially pretty. Jack could not come in on the scrubbed floors. The windows were shining and the pink-edged curtains were freshly crisp and white. Laura and Mary made new starry papers for the shelves, and Ma made vanity cakes.

She made them with beaten eggs and white flour. She dropped them into a kettle of sizzling fat. Each one came up bobbing, and floated till it turned itself over, lifting up its honey-brown, puffy bottom. Then it swelled underneath till it was round, and Ma lifted it out with a fork.

She put every one of those cakes in the cupboard. They were for the party.

Laura and Mary and Ma and Carrie were dressed up and waiting when the guests came walking out from town. Laura had even brushed Jack, though he was always clean and handsome in his white and brown-spotted short fur.

He ran down with Laura to the ford. The girls

came laughing and splashing through the sunny water, all except Nellie. She had to take off her shoes and stockings and she complained that the gravel hurt her feet. She said: 'I don't go barefooted. I have shoes and stockings.'

She was wearing a new dress and big, new hair-ribbon bows.

'Is that Jack?' Christy asked, and they all patted him and said what a good dog he was. But when he politely wagged to Nellie, she said: 'Go away! Don't you touch my dress!'

'Jack wouldn't touch your dress,' Laura said.

They went up the path between the blowing grasses and wild flowers, to the house where Ma was waiting. Mary told her the girls' names one by one, and she smiled her lovely smile and spoke to them. But Nellie smoothed down her new pretty dress and said to Ma:

'Of course I didn't wear my best dress to just a country party.'

Then Laura didn't care what Ma had taught her; she didn't care if Pa punished her. She was going to get even with Nellie for that. Nellie couldn't speak that way to Ma.

Ma only smiled and said: 'It's a very pretty dress, Nellie. We're glad you could come.' But Laura was not going to forgive Nellie.

The girls liked the pretty house. It was so clean and airy, with sweet-smelling breezes blowing through it and the grassy prairies all around. They climbed the ladder and looked at Laura's and Mary's very own attic; none of them had anything like that. But Nellie asked, 'Where are your dolls?'

Laura was not going to show her darling rag Charlotte to Nellie Oleson. She said: 'I don't play with dolls. I play in the creek.'

Then they went outdoors with Jack. Laura showed them the little chicks by the hay-stacks, and they looked at the green garden rows and the thick-growing wheat-field. They ran down the knoll to the low bank of Plum Creek. There was the willow and footbridge, and the water coming out of the plum thicket's shade, running wide and shallow over sparkling pebbles and gurgling under the bridge to the knee-deep pool.

Mary and the big girls came down slowly, bringing Carrie to play with. But Laura and Christy and Maud and Nellie held their skirts up above their knees and went wading into the cool, flowing water. Away through the shallows the minnows went swimming in crowds away from the shouts and splashing.

The big girls took Carrie wading where the water sparkled thin in the sunshine, and gathered pretty pebbles along the creek's edge. The little girls played tag across the footbridge. They ran on the warm grass, and played in the water again. And while they were playing, Laura suddenly thought of what she could do to Nellie.

She led the girls wading near the old crab's home. The noise and splashing had driven him under his rock. She saw his angry claws and browny-green head peeping out, and she crowded Nellie near him. Then she kicked a big splash of water on to his rock and she screamed,

'Oo, Nellie! Nellie, look out!'

The old crab rushed at Nellie's toes, snapping his claws to nip them.

'Run! Run!' Laura screamed, pushing Christy and Maud back towards the bridge, and then she ran after Nellie. Nellie ran screaming straight into the muddy water under the plum thicket. Laura stopped on the gravel and looked back at the crab's rock.

'Wait, Nellie,' she said. 'You stay there.'

'Oh, what was it? What was it? Is he coming?' Nellie asked. She had dropped her dress, and her skirt petticoats were in the muddy water.

'It's an old crab,' Laura told her. 'He cuts big sticks in two with his claws. He could cut our toes right off.'

'Oh, where is he? Is he coming?' Nellie asked.

'You stay there and I'll look,' said Laura, and she went

wading slowly and stopping and looking. The old crab was under his rock again, but Laura did not say so. She waded very slowly all the way to the bridge, while Nellie watched from the plum thicket. Then she waded back and said, 'You can come out now.'

Nellie came out into the clean water. She said she didn't like that horried old creek and wasn't going to play any more. She tried to wash her muddy skirt and then she tried to wash her feet, and then she screamed.

Muddy-brown bloodsuckers were sticking to her legs and her feet. She couldn't wash them off. She tried to pick one off, and then she ran screaming up on the creek bank. There she stood kicking as hard as she could, first one foot and then the other, screaming all the time.

Laura laughed till she fell on the grass and rolled. 'Oh, look, look!' she shouted, laughing. 'See Nellie dance!'

All the girls came running. Mary told Laura to pick those bloodsuckers off Nellie, but Laura didn't listen. She kept on rolling and laughing.

'Laura!' Mary said. 'You get up and pull those things off, or I'll tell Ma.'

Then Laura began to pull the bloodsuckers off Nellie. All the girls watched and screamed while she pulled them out long, and longer, and longer. Nellie cried: 'I don't like your party!' she said. 'I want to go home!'

Ma came hurrying down to the creek to see why they were screaming. She told Nellie not to cry, a few leeches were nothing to cry about. She said it was time now for them all to come to the house.

The table was set prettily with Ma's best white cloth and the blue pitcher full of flowers. The benches were drawn up on either side of it. Shiny tin cups were full of cold, creamy milk from the cellar, and the big platter was heaped with honey-coloured vanity cakes.

The cakes were not sweet, but they were rich and crisp, and hollow inside. Each one was like a great bubble. The crisp bits of it melted on the tongue.

They ate and ate those vanity cakes. They said they had never tasted anything so good, and they asked Ma what they were.

'Vanity cakes,' said Ma. 'Because they are all puffed up, like vanity, with nothing solid inside.'

There were so many vanity cakes that they ate till they could eat no more, and they drank all the sweet, cold milk they could hold. Then the party was over. All the girls but Nellie said thank you for the party. Nellie was still mad.

Laura did not care. Christy squeezed her and said in

her ear, 'I never had such a good time! And it just served Nellie right!'

Deep down inside her Laura felt satisfied when she thought of Nellie dancing on the creek bank.

24

Going to Church

It was Saturday night and Pa sat on the doorstep, smoking his after-supper pipe.

Laura and Mary sat close on either side of him. Ma with Carrie in her lap, rocked gently to and fro, just inside the doorway.

The winds were still. The stars hung low and bright. The dark sky was deep beyond the stars, and Plum Creek talked softly to itself.

'They told me in town this afternoon that there will be preaching in the new church tomorrow,' said Pa. 'I met the home missionary, Reverend Alden, and he wanted us to be sure to come. I told him we would.'

'Oh, Charles,' Ma exclaimed, 'we haven't been to church for so long!'

Laura and Mary had never seen a church. But they knew from Ma's voice that going to church must be better than a party. After a while Ma said, 'I am so glad I finished my new dress.'

'You will look sweet as a posy in it,' Pa told her. 'We must start early.'

Next morning was a hurry. Breakfast was a hurry, work was a hurry, and Ma hurried about dressing herself and Carrie. She called up the ladder in a hurrying voice: 'Come on down, girls. I'll tie your ribbons.'

They hurried down. Then they stood and stared at Ma. She was perfectly beautiful in her new dress. It was black-and-white calico, a narrow stripe of white, then a wider stripe of black lines and white lines no wider than threads. Up the front it was buttoned with black buttons. And the skirt was pulled back and lifted up to puffs and shirrings behind.

Crocheted lace edged the little stand-up collar. Crocheted lace spread out in a bow on Ma's breast, and the gold breast-pin held the collar and the bow. Ma's face was lovely. Her cheeks were flushed and her eyes were bright.

She turned Laura and Mary around and quickly tied the ribbons on their braids. Then she took Carrie's hand. They all went out on the doorstep and Ma locked the door.

Carrie looked like one of the little angel-birds in the Bible. Her dress and her tiny sunbonnet were white and all trimmed with lace. Her eyes were big and solemn; her golden curls hung by her cheeks and peeped from under the bonnet behind.

Then Laura saw her own pink ribbons on Mary's braids. She clapped her hand over her mouth before a word came out. She twisted round and looked down her own back. Mary's blue ribbons were on her braids!

She and Mary looked at each other and did not say a word. Ma, in her hurry, had made a mistake. They hoped she would not notice. Laura was so tired of pink and Mary was so tired of blue. But Mary had to wear blue because her hair was golden and Laura had to wear pink because her hair was brown.

Pa came driving the wagon from the stable. He had brushed Sam and David till they shone in the morning sunshine. They stepped proudly, tossing their heads, and their manes and tails rippled.

There was a clean blanket on the wagon seat and another spread on the bottom of the wagon box. Pa carefully helped Ma climb up over the wheel. He lifted Carrie to Ma's lap. Then he tossed Laura into the wagon box and her braids flew out.

'Oh dear!' Ma exclaimed. 'I put the wrong ribbons on Laura's hair!'

'It'll never be noticed on a trotting horse!' said Pa. So Laura knew she could wear the blue ribbons.

Sitting beside Mary on the clean blanket in the wagon bottom, she pulled her braids over her shoulder. So did

Mary, and they smiled at each other. Laura could see the blue whenever she looked down, and Mary could see the pink.

Pa was whistling, and when Sam and David started he began to sing.

> 'Oh, every Sunday morning
> My wife is by my side
> A-waiting for the wagon,
> And we'll all take a ride!'

'Charles,' Ma said, softly, to remind him that this was Sunday. Then they all sang together,

> 'There is a happy land,
> Far, far away,
> Where saints in glory stand,
> Bright, bright as day!'

Plum Creek came out from the willow shadows and spread wide and flat and twinkling in the sunshine. Sam and David trotted through the sparkling shallows. Glittering drops flew up, and waves splashed from the wheels. Then they were away on the endless prairie.

The wagon rolled softly along the road that hardly

made a mark on the green grasses. Birds sang their morning songs. Bees hummed. Great yellow bumblebees went bumbling from flower to flower, and big grasshoppers flew up and away.

Too soon they came to town. The blacksmith shop was shut and still. The doors of the stores were closed. A few dressed-up men and women, with their dressed-up children, walked along the edges of dusty Main Street. They were all going towards the church.

The church was a new building not far from the schoolhouse. Pa drove towards it through the prairie grass. It was like the schoolhouse, except that on its roof was a tiny room with no walls and nothing in it.

'What's that?' Laura asked.

'Don't point, Laura,' said Ma. 'It's a belfry.'

Pa stopped the wagon against the high porch of the church. He helped Ma out of the wagon, but Laura and Mary just stepped over the side of the wagon box. They all waited there while Pa drove into the shade of the church, unhitched Sam and David and tied them to the wagon box.

People were coming through the grass, climbing the steps and going into the church. There was a solemn, low rustling inside it.

At last Pa came. He took Carrie on his arm and walked

with Ma into the church. Laura and Mary walked softly, close behind them. They all sat in a row on a long bench.

Church was exactly like a schoolhouse, except that it had a strange, large, hollow feeling. Every little noise was loud against the new board walls.

A tall, thin man stood up behind the tall desk on the platform. His clothes were black and his big cravat was black and his hair and the beard that went around his face were dark. His voice was gentle and kind. All the heads bowed down. The man's voice talked to God for a long time, while Laura sat perfectly still and looked at the blue ribbons on her braids.

Suddenly, right beside her, a voice said, 'Come with me.'

Laura almost jumped out of her skin. A pretty lady stood there, smiling out of soft blue eyes. The lady said again, 'Come with me, little girls. We are going to have a Sunday-school class.'

Ma nodded at them, so Laura and Mary slid down from the bench. They had not known there was going to be school on Sunday.

The lady led them to a corner. All the girls from school were there, looking questions at one another. The lady pulled benches around to make a square pen. She sat down and took Laura and Christy beside her. When the others were settled on the square of benches, the lady said her name was Mrs Tower, and she asked their names. Then she said, 'Now, I'm going to tell you a story!'

Laura was very pleased. But Mrs Tower began, 'It is all about a little baby, born long ago in Egypt. His name was Moses.'

So Laura did not listen any more. She knew all about Moses in the bulrushes. Even Carrie knew that.

After the story, Mrs Tower smiled more than ever, and said. 'Now we'll all learn a Bible verse! Won't that be nice?'

'Yes, ma'am,' they all said. She told a Bible verse to each girl in turn. They were to remember the verses and repeat them to her next Sunday. That was their Sunday-school lesson.

When it was Laura's turn, Mrs Tower cuddled her and smiled almost as warm and sweet as Ma. She said, 'My very littlest girl must have a very small lesson. It will be the shortest verse in the Bible!'

Then Laura knew what it was. But Mrs Tower's eyes smiled and she said, 'It is just three words!' She said them, and asked, 'Now do you think you can remember that for a whole week?'

Laura was surprised at Mrs Tower. Why, she remembered long Bible verses and whole songs! But she did not want to hurt Mrs Tower's feelings. So she said, 'Yes, ma'am.'

'That's my little girl!' Mrs Tower said. But Laura was Ma's little girl. 'I'll tell you again, to help you remember. Just three words,' said Mrs Tower. 'Now can you say them after me?'

Laura squirmed.

'Try,' Mrs Tower urged her. Laura's head bowed lower and she whispered the verse.

'That's right!' Mrs Tower said. 'Now will you do your best to remember, and tell me next Sunday?'

Laura nodded.

After that everyone stood up. They all opened their mouths and tried to sing 'Jerusalem, the Golden.' Not many of them knew the words or the tune. Miserable squiggles went up Laura's backbone and the insides of her ears crinkled. She was glad when they all sat down again.

Then the tall, thin man stood up and talked.

Laura thought he never would stop talking. She looked through the open windows at butterflies going where they pleased. She watched the grasses blowing in the wind. She listened to the wind whining thin along the edges of the roof. She looked at the blue hair ribbons. She looked at each of her finger nails and admired how the fingers of her hands would fit together. She struck her fingers out straight, so they looked like the corner of a log house. She looked at the underneath of shingles, overhead. Her legs ached from dangling still.

At last every one stood up and tried again to sing. When that was over, there was no more. They could go home.

The tall thin man was standing by the door. He was the Reverend Alden. He shook Ma's hand and he shook Pa's hand and they talked. Then he bent down, and he shook Laura's hand.

His teeth smiled in his dark beard. His eyes were warm and blue. He asked, 'Did you like Sunday-school, Laura?'

Suddenly Laura did like it. She said, 'Yes, sir.'

'Then you must come every Sunday!' he said. 'We'll expect you.' And Laura knew he really would expect her. He would not forget.

On the way home Pa said, 'Well, Caroline, it's pleasant to be with a crowd of people all trying to do the right thing, same as we are.'

'Yes, Charles,' Ma said, thankfully. 'It will be a pleasure to look forward to, all week.'

Pa turned on the seat and asked, 'How do you girls like the first time you ever went to church?'

'They can't sing,' said Laura.

Pa's great laugh rang out. Then he explained, 'There was nobody to pitch the hymn with a tuning-fork.'

'Nowadays, Charles,' said Ma, 'people have hymn books.'

'Well, maybe we'll be able to afford some, some day,' Pa said.

After that they went to Sunday-school every Sunday. Three or four Sundays they went to Sunday-school, and then again the Reverend Alden was there, and that was a church Sunday. The Reverend Alden lived at his real church, in the East. He could not travel all the way to this church every Sunday. This was his home missionary church, in the West.

There were no more long, dull, tiresome Sundays, because there was always Sunday-school to go to, and to talk about afterwards. The best Sundays were the Sundays when the Reverend Alden was there. He always remembered Laura, and she remembered him betweentimes. He called Laura and Mary his 'little country girls'.

Then one Sunday while Pa and Ma and Mary and Laura were all sitting at the dinner table, talking about that day's Sunday-school, Pa said, 'If I'm going to keep on going out among dressed-up folks I must get a pair of new boots. Look.'

He stretched out his foot. His mended boot was cracked clear across the toes.

They all looked at his red knitted sock showing through that gaping slit. The edges of leather were thin and curling back between little cracks. Pa said, 'It won't hold another patch.'

'Oh, I wanted you to get boots, Charles,' Ma said. 'And you brought home that calico for my dress.'

Pa made up his mind. 'I'll get me a new pair when I go to town next Saturday. They will cost three dollars, but we'll make out somehow till I harvest the wheat.'

All that week Pa was making hay. He had helped put up Mr Nelson's hay and earned the use of Mr Nelson's fine, quick mowing-machine. He said it was wonderful weather for making hay. He had never known such a dry, sunny summer.

Laura hated to go to school. She wanted to be out in the hay-field with Pa, watching the marvellous machine with its long knives snickety-snicking behind the wheels, cutting through great swathes of grass.

Saturday morning she went to the field on the wagon, and helped Pa bring in the last load of hay. They looked at the wheat-field, standing up taller than Laura above the mown land. Its level top was rough with wheat-heads, bent with the weight of ripening wheat. They picked three long, fat ones and took them to the house to show Ma.

When that crop was harvested, Pa said, they'd be out of debt and have more money than they knew what to do with. He'd have a buggy, Ma would have a silk dress, they'd all have new shoes and eat beef every Sunday.

After dinner he put on a clean shirt and took three dollars out of the fiddle-box. He was going to town to get his new boots. He walked, because the horses had been working all that week and he left them at home to rest.

It was late that afternoon when Pa came walking home, Laura saw him on the knoll and she and Jack ran up from the old crab's home in the creek and into the house behind him.

Ma turned around from the stove, where she was taking the Saturday baking of bread out of the oven.

'Where are your boots, Charles?' she asked.

'Well, Caroline,' Pa said. 'I saw Brother Alden and he told me he couldn't raise money enough to put a bell in the belfry. The folks in town had all given every cent they could, and he lacked just three dollars. So I gave him the money.'

'Oh, Charles!' was all Ma said.

Pa looked down at his cracked boot. 'I'll patch it,' he said. 'I can make it hold together somehow. And do you know, we'll hear that church bell ringing clear out here.'

Ma turned quickly back to the stove, and Laura went quietly out and sat down on the step. Her throat hurt her. She did so want Pa to have good new boots.

'Never mind, Caroline,' she heard Pa saying. 'It's not long to wait till I harvest the wheat.'

25

The Glittering Cloud

Now the wheat was almost ready to cut. Every day Pa looked at it. Every night he talked about it, and showed Laura some long, stiff wheat-heads. The plump grains were getting harder in their little husks. Pa said the weather was perfect for ripening wheat.

'If this keeps up,' he said, 'we'll start harvesting next week.'

The weather was very hot. The thin, high sky was too hot to look at. Air rose up in waves from the whole prairie, as it does from a hot stove. In the schoolhouse the children panted like lizards, and the sticky pine-juice dripped down the board walls.

Saturday morning Laura went walking with Pa to look at the wheat. It was almost as tall as Pa. He lifted her on to his shoulder so that she could see over the heavy, bending tops. The field was greeny gold.

At the dinner table Pa told Ma about it. He had never seen such a crop. There were forty bushels to the acre, and wheat was a dollar a bushel. They were rich now. This was a wonderful country. Now they could have anything they wanted. Laura listened and thought, now Pa would get his new boots.

She sat facing the open door and the sunshine streaming through it. Something seemed to dim the sunshine. Laura rubbed her eyes and looked again. The sunshine really was dim. It grew dimmer until there was no sunshine.

'I do believe a storm is coming up,' said Ma. 'There must be a cloud over the sun.'

Pa got up quickly and went to the door. A storm might hurt the wheat. He looked out, then he went out.

The light was queer. It was not like the changed light before a storm. The air did not press down as it did before a storm. Laura was frightened, she did not know why.

She ran outdoors, where Pa stood looking up at the sky. Ma and Mary came out, too, and Pa asked, 'What do you make of that, Caroline?'

A cloud was over the sun. It was not like any cloud they had ever seen before. It was a cloud of something like snowflakes, but they were larger than snowflakes, and thin and glittering. Light shone through each flickering particle.

There was no wind. The grasses were still and the hot air did not stir, but the edge of the cloud came on across the sky faster than wind. The hair stood up on Jack's neck. All at once he made a frightful sound up at that cloud, a growl and a whine.

Plunk! something hit Laura's head and fell to the ground. She looked down and saw the largest grasshopper she had ever seen. Then huge brown grasshoppers were hitting the ground all around her, hitting her head and her face and her arms. They came thudding down like hail.

The cloud was hailing grasshoppers. The cloud *was* grasshoppers. Their bodies hid the sun and made darkness. Their thin, large wings gleamed and glittered. The rasping whirring of their wings filled the whole air and they hit the ground and the house with the noise of a hailstorm.

Laura tried to beat them off. Their claws clung to her skin and her dress. They looked at her with bulging eyes, turning their heads this way and that. Mary ran screaming into the house. Grasshoppers covered the ground, there was not one bare bit to step on. Laura had to step on grasshoppers and they smashed squirming and slimy under her feet.

Ma was slamming the windows shut, all around the house. Pa came and stood just inside the front door, looking out. Laura and Jack stood close beside him. Grasshoppers beat down from the sky and swarmed thick over the ground. Their long wings were folded and their strong legs took them hopping everywhere. The air whirred and the roof went on sounding like a roof in a hailstorm.

Then Laura heard another sound, one big sound made of tiny nips and snips and gnawings.

'The wheat!' Pa shouted. He dashed out the back door and ran towards the wheat-field.

The grasshoppers were eating. You could not hear one grasshopper eat, unless you listened very carefully while you held him and fed him grass. Millions and millions of grasshoppers were eating now. You could hear the millions of jaws biting and chewing.

Pa came running back to the stable. Through the window Laura saw him hitching Sam and David to the wagon. He began pitching old dirty hay from the manure-pile into the wagon, as fast as he could. Ma ran out, took the other pitchfork and helped him. Then he drove away to the wheat-field and Ma followed the wagon.

Pa drove around the field, throwing out little piles of stuff as he went. Ma stooped over one, then a thread of smoke rose from it and spread. Ma lighted pile after pile. Laura watched till a smudge of smoke hid the field and Ma and Pa and the wagon.

Grasshoppers were still falling from the sky. The light was still dim because grasshoppers covered the sun.

Ma came back to the house, and in the closed lean-to she took off her dress and her petticoats and killed the grasshoppers she shook out of them. She had lighted fires all around the wheat-field. Perhaps smoke would keep the grasshoppers from eating the wheat.

Ma and Mary and Laura were quiet in the shut, smothery house. Carrie was so little that she cried, even in Ma's arms. She cried herself to sleep. Through the walls came the sound of grasshoppers eating.

The darkness went away. The sun shone again. All over the ground was a crawling, hopping mass of grasshoppers. They were eating all the soft, short grass off the knoll. The tall prairie grasses swayed and bent and fell.

'Oh, look,' Laura said, low, at the window.

They were eating the willow tops. The willows' leaves were thin and bare twigs stuck out. Then whole branches

were bare, and knobby with masses of grasshoppers.

'I don't want to look any more,' Mary said, and she went away from the window. Laura did not want to look any more, either, but she could not stop looking.

The hens were funny. The two hens and their gawky pullets were eating grasshoppers with all their might. They were used to stretching their necks out low and running fast after grasshoppers and not catching them. Every time they stretched out now, they got a grasshopper right then. They were surprised. They kept stretching out their necks and trying to run in all directions at once.

'Well, we won't have to buy feed for the hens,' said Ma. 'There's no great loss without some gain.'

The green garden rows were wilting down. The potatoes, the carrots, the beets and beans were being eaten away. The long leaves were eaten off the cornstalks, and the tassels, and the ears of young corn in their green husks fell covered with grasshoppers.

There was nothing anybody could do about it.

Smoke still hid the wheat-field. Sometimes Laura saw Pa moving dimly in it. He stirred up the smouldering fires and thick smoke hid him again.

When it was time to go for Spot, Laura put on stockings and shoes and a shawl. Spot was standing in the old ford of Plum Creek, shaking her skin and switching her tail. The herd went mournfully lowing beyond the old dugout. Laura was sure that cattle could not eat grass so full of grasshoppers. If the grasshoppers ate all the grass, the cattle would starve.

Grasshoppers were thick under her petticoats and on her dress and shawl. She kept striking them off her face and hands. Her shoes and Spot's feet crunched grasshoppers.

Ma came out in a shawl to do the milking. Laura helped her. They could not keep grasshoppers out of the milk. Ma had brought a cloth to cover the pail but they could not keep it covered while they milked into it. Ma skimmed out the grasshoppers with a tin cup.

Grasshoppers went into the house with them. Their clothes were full of grasshoppers. Some jumped on to the hot stove where Mary was starting supper. Ma covered the food till they had chased and smashed every grasshopper. She swept them up and shovelled them into the stove.

Pa came into the house long enough to eat supper while Sam and David were eating theirs. Ma did not ask him what was happening to the wheat. She only smiled and said: 'Don't worry, Charles. We've always got along.'

Pa's throat rasped and Ma said: 'Have another cup of tea, Charles. It will help get the smoke out of your throat.'

When Pa had drunk the tea, he went back to the wheat-field with another load of old hay and manure.

In bed, Laura and Mary could still hear the whirring and snipping and chewing. Laura felt claws crawling on her. There were no grasshoppers in bed, but she could not brush the feeling off her arms and cheeks. In the dark she saw grasshoppers' bulging eyes and felt their claws crawling until she went to sleep.

Pa was not downstairs next morning. All night he had been working to keep the smoke over the wheat, and he did not come to breakfast. He was still working.

The whole prairie was changed. The grasses did not wave; they had fallen in ridges. The rising sun made all the prairie rough with shadows where the tall grasses had sunk against each other.

The willow trees were bare. In the plum thickets only a few plumpits hung to the leafless branches. The nipping, clicking, gnawing sound of the grasshoppers' eating was still going on.

At noon Pa came driving the wagon out of the smoke. He put Sam and David into the stable, and slowly came to the house. His face was black with smoke and his eyeballs were red. He hung his hat on the nail behind the door and sat down at the table.

'It's no use, Caroline,' he said. 'Smoke won't stop them. They keep dropping down through it and hopping in from all sides. The wheat is falling now. They're cutting it off like a scythe. And eating it, straw and all.'

He put his elbows on the table and hid his face with his hands. Laura and Mary sat still. Only Carrie on her high stool rattled her spoon and reached her little hand towards the bread. She was too young to understand.

'Never mind, Charles,' Ma said. 'We've been through hard times before.'

Laura looked down at Pa's patched boots under the table and her throat swelled and ached. Pa could not have new boots now.

Pa's hands came down from his face and he picked up

his knife and fork. His beard smiled, but his eyes would not twinkle. They were dull and dim.

'Don't worry, Caroline,' he said. 'We did all we could, and we'll pull through somehow.'

Then Laura remembered that the new house was not paid for. Pa had said he would pay for it when he harvested the wheat.

It was a quiet meal, and when it was over Pa lay down on the floor and went to sleep. Ma slipped a pillow under his head and laid her finger on her lips to tell Laura and Mary to be still.

They took Carrie into the bedroom and kept her quiet with their paper dolls. The only sound was the sound of the grasshoppers' eating.

Day after day the grasshoppers kept on eating. They ate all the wheat and the oats. They ate every green thing – all the garden and all the prairie grass.

'Oh, Pa, what will the rabbits do?' Laura asked. 'And the poor birds?'

'Look around you, Laura,' Pa said.

The rabbits had all gone away. The little birds of the grass tops were gone. The birds that were left were eating grasshoppers. And prairie hens ran with outstretched necks, gobbling grasshoppers.

When Sunday came, Pa and Laura and Mary walked to

Sunday-school. The sun shone so bright and hot that Ma said she would stay at home with Carrie, and Pa left Sam and David in the shady stable.

There had been no rain for so long that Laura walked across Plum Creek on dry stones. The whole prairie was bare and brown. Millions of brown grasshoppers whirred low over it. Not a green thing was in sight anywhere.

All the way, Laura and Mary brushed off grasshoppers. When they came to the church, brown grasshoppers were thick on their petticoats. They lifted their skirts and brushed them off before they went in. But careful as they were, the grasshoppers had spit tobacco-juice on their best Sunday dresses.

Nothing would take out the horrid stains. They would have to wear their best dresses with the brown spots on them.

Many people in town were going back East. Christy and Cassie had to go. Laura said goodbye to Christy and Mary said goodbye to Cassie, their best friends.

They did not go to school any more. They must save their shoes for winter and they could not bear to walk barefooted on grasshoppers. School would be ended soon, anyway, and Ma said she would teach them through the winter so they would not be behind their classes when school opened again next spring.

Pa worked for Mr Nelson and earned the use of Mr Nelson's plough. He began to plough the bare wheatfield, to make it ready for next year's wheat crop.

26

Grasshopper Eggs

One day Laura and Jack wandered down to the creek. Mary liked to sit and read and work sums on the slate, but Laura grew tired of that. Outdoors was so miserable that she did not much like to play, either.

Plum Creek was almost dry. Only a little water seeped through the pebbly sand. The bare willow did not shade the footbridge now. Under the leafless plum thicket the water was scummy. The old crab had gone away.

The dry earth was hot, the sunshine was scorching and the sky was a brassy colour. The whirring of grasshoppers sounded like heat. There were no good smells any more.

Then Laura saw a queer thing. All over the knoll grasshoppers were sitting still with their tails down in the ground. They did not stir, even when Laura poked them.

She poked one away from the hole in which it was sitting, and with a stick she dug out of the hole a grey thing. It was like a fat worm, but it was not alive. She did not know what it was. Jack snuffed at it, and wondered, too.

Laura started towards the wheat-field to ask Pa about it. But Pa was not ploughing. Sam and David were standing still with the plough, and Pa was walking on the unploughed ground, looking at it. Then Laura saw him go to the plough and lift it out of the furrow. He went, driving Sam and David towards the stable with the idle plough.

Laura knew that only something dreadful would make Pa stop work in the middle of the morning. She went as fast as she could to the stable. Sam and David were in their stalls and Pa was hanging up their sweaty harness. He came out, and did not smile at Laura. She tagged slowly after him into the house.

Ma looked up at him and said, 'Charles! What is the matter now?'

'The grasshoppers are laying their eggs,' said Pa. 'The ground's honeycombed with them. Look at the dooryard, and you'll see the pits where the eggs are buried a couple of inches deep. All over the wheat-field. Everywhere. You can't put your finger down between them. Look here.'

He took one of those grey things from his pocket and held it out on his hand.

'That's one of 'em, a pod of grasshopper eggs. I've been cutting them open. There's thirty-five or forty eggs in every pod. There's a pod in every hole. There's eight or ten holes to the square foot. All over this whole country.'

Ma dropped down in a chair and let her hands fall helpless at her sides.

'We've got no more chance of making a crop next year than we have of flying,' said Pa. 'When those eggs hatch, there won't be a green thing left in this part of the world.'

'Oh, Charles!' Ma said. 'What will we do?'

Pa slumped down on a bench and said, 'I don't know.'

Mary's braids swung over the edge of the ladder hole and her face looked down between them. She looked anxiously at Laura and Laura looked up at her. Then Mary backed down the ladder without a sound. She stood close beside Laura, backed against the wall.

Pa straightened up. His dim eyes brightened with a fierce light, not like the twinkle Laura had always seen in them.

'But I do know this, Caroline,' he said. 'No pesky mess of grasshoppers can best us! We'll do something! You'll see! We'll get along somehow.'

'Yes, Charles,' said Ma.

'Why not?' said Pa. 'We're healthy, we've got a roof over our heads; we're better off than lots of folks. You get an early dinner, Caroline. I'm going to town. I'll find something to do. Don't you worry!'

While he was gone to town, Ma and Mary and Laura planned a fine supper for him. Ma scalded a pan of sour milk and made pretty white balls of cottage cheese. Mary and Laura sliced cold boiled potatoes and Ma made a sauce

178

for them. There were bread and butter and milk besides.

Then they washed and combed their hair. They put on their best dresses and their hair ribbons. They put Carrie's white dress on her, and brushed her hair and tied the string of Indian beads around her neck. They were all waiting when Pa came up the grasshoppery knoll.

That was a merry supper. When they had eaten every bit of it, Pa pushed back his plate and said 'Well, Caroline.'

'Yes, Charles?' Ma said.

'Here's the way out,' said Pa. 'I'm going *east* tomorrow morning.'

'Oh, Charles! No!' Ma cried out.

'It's all right, Laura,' Pa said. He meant, 'Don't cry,' and Laura did not cry.

'It's harvest time back there,' Pa told them. 'The grasshoppers went only about a hundred miles east of here. Beyond that there's crops. It's the only chance to get a job, and all the men in the West are heading for those jobs. I've got to get there quick.'

'If you think it's for the best,' Ma said, 'the girls and I can get along. But, oh, Charles, it will be such a long walk for you!'

'Shucks! What's a couple of hundred miles?' said Pa. But he glanced at his old patched boots. Laura knew he was wondering if they would last to walk so far. 'A couple of hundred miles don't amount to anything!' he said.

Then he took his fiddle out of its box. He played for a long time in the twilight, while Laura and Mary sat close to him and Ma rocked Carrie near by.

He played 'Dixie Land,' and 'We'll Rally Round the Flag, Boys!' He played 'All the Blue Bonnets Are Over the Border,' and

Oh, Susanna, don't you cry for me!
I'm going to California
With my washpan on my knee!

He played 'The Campbells Are Coming, Hurrah! Hurrah!' Then he played 'Life Let Us Cherish.' And he put away the fiddle. He must go to bed early, to get an early start in the morning.

'Take good care of the old fiddle, Caroline,' he said. 'It puts heart into a man.'

After breakfast, at dawn, Pa kissed them all and went away. His extra shirt and pair of socks were rolled in his jumper and slung on his shoulder. Just before he crossed Plum Creek he looked back and waved. Then he went on, all the way out of sight, without turning again. Jack stood pressed close against Laura.

They all stood still for a moment after Pa was gone.

Then Ma said, cheerfully, 'We have to take care of everything now, girls. Mary and Laura, you hurry with the cow to meet the herd.'

She went briskly into the house with Carrie while Laura and Mary ran to let Spot out of the stable and drive her towards the creek. No prairie grass was left, and the hungry cattle could only wander along the creek banks, eating willow sprouts and plum brush and a little dead, dry grass left from last summer.

27

Rain

Everything was flat and dull when Pa was gone. Laura and Mary could not even count the days till he would come back. They could only think of him walking farther and farther away in his patched boots.

Jack was a sober dog now and his nose was turning grey. Often he looked at the empty road where Pa had gone, and sighed, and lay down to watch it. But he did not really hope that Pa could come.

The dead, eaten prairie was flat under the hot sky. Dust devils rose up and whirled across it. The far-away edge of it seemed to crawl like a snake. Ma said that was caused by the heat waves of the air.

The only shade was in the house. There were no leaves on willows or plum thickets. Plum Creek dried up. There was only a little water in its pools. The well was dry, and the old spring by the dugout was only a drip. Ma set a pail under it, to fill during the night. In the morning she brought it to the house and left another pail to fill during the day.

When the morning work was done, Ma and Mary and

182

Laura and Carrie sat in the house. The scorching winds whizzed by and the hungry cattle never stopped lowing.

Spot was thin. Her hip joints stuck up sharp, all her ribs showed, and there were hollows around her eyes. All day she went mooing with the other cattle, looking for something to eat. They had eaten all the little bushes along the creek and gnawed the willow branches as high as they could reach. Spot's milk was bitter, and every day she gave less of it.

Sam and David stood in the stable. They could not have all the hay they wanted, because the hay-stacks must last till next spring. When Laura led them down the dry creek-bed to the old swimming-hole, they curled their noses at the warm, scummy water. But they had to drink it. Cows and horses had to bear things, too.

Saturday, Laura went to the Nelsons' to see if a letter had come from Pa. She went along the little path beyond the footbridge. It did not go wandering forever through pleasant places. It went to Mr Nelson's.

Mr Nelson's house was long and low and its board walls were whitewashed. His long, low sod stable had a thick roof made of hay. They did not look like Pa's house and Pa's stable. They cuddled to the ground, under a slope of the prairie, and they looked as if they spoke Norwegian.

The house was shining clean inside. The big bed was

plumped high with feathers and the pillows were high and fat. On the wall hung a beautiful picture of a lady dressed in blue. Its frame was thick gold, and bright pink mosquito-netting covered the lady and the frame, to keep the flies off.

There was no letter from Pa. Mrs Nelson said that Mr Nelson would ask again at the post-office, next Saturday.

'Thank you, ma'am,' Laura said, and she hurried fast along the path. Then she walked slowly across the foot bridge, and more and more slowly up the knoll.

Ma said, 'Never mind, girls. There will be a letter next Saturday.'

But next Saturday there was no letter.

They did not go to Sunday-school any more. Carrie could not walk so far and she was too heavy for Ma to carry. Laura and Mary must save their shoes. They could not go to Sunday-school barefooted, and if they wore out their shoes they would have no shoes next winter.

So on Sundays they put on their best dresses, but not their shoes or ribbons. Mary and Laura said their Bible verses to Ma, and she read to them from the Bible.

One Sunday she read to them about the plague of locusts, long ago in Bible times. Locusts were grasshoppers. Ma read:

'And the locusts went up over the land of Egypt, and rested in all the coasts of Egypt; very grievous were they.

'For they covered the face of the whole earth, so that the land was darkened; and they did eat every herb of the land, and all the fruits of the trees which the hail had left; and there remained not any green thing on the trees, or in the herbs of the field, through all the land of Egypt.'

Laura knew how true that was. When she repeated those verses she thought, 'through all the land of Minnesota.'

Then Ma read the promise that God made to good people, 'to bring them out of that land to a good land and a large, unto a land flowing with milk and honey.'

'Oh, where is that, Ma?' Mary asked, and Laura asked, 'How could land flow with milk and honey?' She did not want to walk in milky, sticky honey.

Ma rested the big Bible on her knees and thought. Then she said, 'Well, your Pa thinks it will be right here in Minnesota.'

'How could it be?' Laura asked.

'Maybe it will be, if we stick it out,' said Ma. 'Well, Laura, if good milch cows were eating grass all over this land, they would give a great deal of milk, and then the land would be flowing with milk. Bees would get honey out of all the wild flowers that grow out of the land, and then the land would be flowing with honey.'

'Oh,' Laura said. 'I'm glad we wouldn't have to walk in it.'

Carrie beat the Bible with her little fists and cried: 'I'm hot! I'm pricky!' Ma picked her up but she pushed at Ma and whimpered, 'You're hot!'

Poor little Carrie's skin was red with heat rash. Laura and Mary were sweltering inside their underwaists and drawers, and petticoat-waists and petticoat, and long-

sleeved, high-necked dresses with tight waistbands around their middles. The backs of their necks were smothering under their braids.

Carrie wanted a drink, but she pushed the cup away and made a face and said, 'Nasty!'

'You'd better drink it,' Mary told her. 'I want a cold drink, too, but there isn't any.'

'I wish I had a drink of well water,' said Laura.

'I wish I had an icicle,' said Mary.

Then Laura said, 'I wish I was an Indian and didn't have to wear clothes.'

'Laura!' said Ma. 'And on Sunday!'

Laura thought, 'Well, I do!' The wood smell of the house was a hot smell. On all the brown streaks in the boards the juice was dripping down sticky and drying in hard yellow beads. The hot wind never stopped whizzing by and the cattle never stopped mourning, 'Moo-oo, moo-oo.' Jack turned on his side and groaned a long sigh.

Ma sighed, too, and said, 'Seems to me I'd give almost anything for a breath of air.'

At that very minute a breath of air came into the house. Carrie stopped whimpering. Jack lifted up his head. Ma said, 'Girls, did you –' Then another cool breath came.

Ma went out through the lean-to, to the shady end of the house. Laura scampered after her, and Mary came leading Carrie. Outdoors was like a baking-oven. The hot air came scorching against Laura's face.

In the northwest sky there was a cloud. It was small in the enormous, brassy sky. But it was a cloud, and it made a streak of shade on the prairie. The shadow seemed to move, but perhaps that was only the heat waves. No, it really was coming nearer.

'Oh, please, please, please!' Laura kept saying, silently, with all her might. They all stood shading their eyes and looking at that cloud and its shadow.

The cloud kept coming nearer. It grew larger. It was a thick, dark streak in the air above the prairie. Its edge rolled and swelled in big puffs. Now gusts of cool air came, mixed with gusts hotter than ever.

All over the prairie, dust devils rose up wild and wicked, whirling their dust arms. The sun still burned on the house and the stable and the cracked, pitted earth. The shadow of the cloud was far away.

Suddenly a fire-white streak zigzagged, and a grey curtain fell from the cloud and hung there, hiding the sky beyond it. That was rain. Then a growl of thunder came.

'It's too far away, girls,' Ma said. 'I'm afraid it won't get to us. But, anyway, the air's cooler.'

A smell of rain came on streaks of coolness through the hot wind.

'Oh, maybe it will get to us, Ma! Maybe it will!' Laura said. Inside themselves they were all saying, 'Please, please, please!'

The wind blew cooler. Slowly, slowly, the cloud shadow grew larger. Now the cloud spread wide in the sky. Suddenly a shadow rushed across the flat land and up the knoll, and fast after it came the marching rain. It came up the knoll like millions of tiny trampling feet, and rain poured down on the house and on Ma and Mary and Laura and Carrie.

'Get in, quick!' Ma exclaimed.

The lean-to was noisy with rain on its roof. Cool air blew through it into the smothery house. Ma opened the front door. She fastened back the curtains and opened every window.

A sick smell steamed up from the ground, but the rain poured down and washed it away. Rain drummed on the roof, rain poured from the eaves. Rain washed the air and made it good to breathe. Sweet air rushed through the house. It lifted the heaviness out of Laura's head and made her skin feel good.

Streams of muddy water ran swiftly over the hard ground. They poured into its cracks and filled them up. They dimpled and swirled over the pits where the grasshoppers' eggs were and left smooth mud there. Overhead the lightning flickered sharp and thunder crashed.

Carrie clapped her hands and shouted; Mary and Laura danced and laughed. Jack wiggled and scampered like a puppy; he looked out at the rain from every window, and when the thunder banged and crashed he growled at it, 'Who's afraid of you!'

'I do believe it is going to last till sunset,' Ma said.

Just before sunset the rain went away. Down across Plum Creek and away across the prairie to the east it went, leaving only a few sparkling drops falling in the sunshine. Then the cloud turned purple and red and curled gold edges against the clear sky. The sun sank and the stars came out. The air was cool and the earth was damp and grateful.

The only thing that Laura wished was that Pa could be there.

Next day the sun rose burning hot. The sky was brassy and the winds were scorching. And before night tiny thin spears of grass were pricking up from the ground.

In a few days there was a green streak across the brown prairie. Grass came up where the rain had fallen, and the hungry cattle grazed there. Every morning Laura put Sam and David on picket lines so they could eat the good grass, too.

The cattle stopped bawling. Spot's bones did not show

any more. She gave more milk, and it was sweet, good milk. The knoll was green again, and the willows and the plums were putting out tiny leaves.

28

The Letter

All day long Laura missed Pa, and at night when the wind blew lonesomely over the dark land, she felt hollow and aching.

At first she talked about him; she wondered how far he had walked that day; she hoped his old, patched boots were lasting; she wondered where he was camping that night. Later she did not speak about him to Ma. Ma was thinking about him all the time and she did not like to talk about it. She did not like even to count the days till Saturday.

'The time will go faster,' she said, 'if we think of other things.'

All day Saturday they hoped that Mr Nelson was finding a letter from Pa at the post-office in town. Laura and Jack went far along the prairie road to wait for Mr Nelson's wagon. The grasshoppers had eaten everything, and now they were going away, not in one big cloud as they had come but in little, short-flying clouds. Still, millions of grasshoppers were left.

There was no letter from Pa. 'Never mind,' Ma said. 'One will come.'

Once when Laura was slowly coming up the knoll without a letter, she thought, 'Suppose no letter ever comes?'

She tried not to think that again. But she did. One day she looked at Mary and knew that Mary was thinking it, too.

That night Laura could not bear it any longer. She asked Ma, 'Pa will come home, won't he?'

'Of course, Pa will come home!' Ma exclaimed. Then Laura and Mary knew that Ma, too, was afraid that something had happened to Pa.

Perhaps his boots had fallen to pieces and he was limping barefooted. Perhaps cattle had hurt him. Perhaps a train had hit him. He had not taken his gun; perhaps wolves had got him. Maybe in dark woods at night a panther had leaped on him from a tree.

The next Saturday afternoon, when Laura and Jack were starting to meet Mr Nelson, she saw him coming across the footbridge. Something white was in his hand. Laura flew down the knoll. The white thing was a letter.

'Oh, thank you! Thank you!' Laura said. She ran to the house so fast that she could not breathe. Ma was washing Carrie's face. She took the letter in her shaking wet hands, and sat down.

'It's from Pa,' she said. Her hand shook so she could

hardly take a hairpin from her hair. She slit the envelope and drew out the letter. She unfolded it, and there was a piece of paper money.

'Pa's all right,' Ma said. She snatched her apron up to her face and cried.

Her wet face came out of the apron shining with joy. She kept wiping her eyes while she read the letter to Mary and Laura.

Pa had had to walk three hundred miles before he found a job. Now he was working in the wheat-fields and getting a dollar a day. He sent Ma five dollars and kept three for new boots. Crops were good where he was, and if Ma and the girls were making out all right, he would stay there as long as the work lasted.

They missed him and wanted him to come home. But he was safe, and already he had new boots. They were very happy that day.

29

The Darkest Hour is Just Before Dawn

Now the winds blew cooler and the sun was not so hot at noon. Mornings were chilly, and the grasshoppers hopped feebly until the sunshine warmed them.

One morning a thick frost covered the ground. It coated every twig and chip with a white fuzz and it burned Laura's bare feet. She saw millions of grasshoppers sitting perfectly stiff.

In a few days there was not one grasshopper left anywhere.

Winter was near, and Pa had not come. The wind was sharp. It did not whizz any more; it shrieked and wailed. The sky was grey and a cold grey rain fell. The rain turned to snow, and still Pa did not come.

Laura had to wear shoes when she went outdoors. They hurt her feet. She did not know why. Those shoes had never hurt her feet before. Mary's shoes hurt Mary's feet, too.

All the wood that Pa had chopped was gone, and Mary and Laura picked up the scattered chips. The cold bit their noses and their fingers while they pried the last chips from the frozen ground. Wrapped in shawls, they went searching under the willows, picking up the little dead branches that made a poor fire.

Then one afternoon Mrs Nelson came visiting. She brought her baby Anna with her.

Mrs Nelson was plump and pretty. Her hair was as golden as Mary's, her eyes were blue, and when she laughed, as she often did, she showed rows of very white teeth. Laura liked Mrs Nelson, but she was not glad to see Anna.

Anna was a little larger than Carrie but she could not understand a word that Laura or Mary said, and they could not understand her. She talked Norwegian. It was no fun to play with her, and in the summertime Mary and Laura ran down to the creek when Mrs Nelson and Anna came. But it was cold. They must stay in the warm house and play with Anna. Ma said so.

'Now girls,' Ma said, 'go get your dolls and play nicely with Anna.'

Laura brought the box of paper dolls that Ma had cut out of wrapping-paper, and they sat down to play on the floor by the open oven door. Anna laughed when she saw the paper dolls. She grabbed into the box, took out a paper lady, and tore her in two.

Laura and Mary were horrified. Carrie stared with round eyes. Ma and Mrs Nelson went on talking and did not see Anna waving the halves of the paper lady and laughing. Laura put the cover on the paper-doll box, but in a little while Anna was tired of the torn paper lady and wanted another. Laura did not know what to do, and neither did Mary.

If Anna did not get what she wanted she bawled. She was little and she was company and they must not make her cry. But if she got the paper dolls she would tear them all up. Then Mary whispered, 'Get Charlotte. She can't hurt Charlotte.'

Laura scurried up the ladder while Mary kept Anna quiet. Darling Charlotte lay in her box under the eaves, smiling with her red yarn mouth and her shoe-button eyes. Laura lifted her carefully and smoothed her wavy black-yarn hair and her skirts. Charlotte had no feet, and her hands were only stitched on the flat ends of her arms, because she was a rag doll. But Laura loved her dearly.

Charlotte had been Laura's very own since Christmas morning long ago in the Big Woods of Wisconsin.

Laura carried her down the ladder, and Anna shouted for her. Laura put Charlotte carefully in Anna's arms. Anna hugged her tight. But hugging could not hurt Charlotte. Laura watched anxiously while Anna tugged at Charlotte's shoe-button eyes and pulled her wavy yarn hair, and even banged her against the floor. But Anna could not really hurt Charlotte, and Laura meant to straighten her skirts and her hair when Anna went away.

At last that long visit was ended. Mrs Nelson was going and taking Anna. Then a terrible thing happened. Anna would not give up Charlotte.

Perhaps she thought Charlotte was hers. Maybe she told her mother that Laura had given her Charlotte. Mrs Nelson smiled. Laura tried to take Charlotte, and Anna howled.

'I want my doll!' Laura said. But Anna hung on to Charlotte and kicked and bawled.

'For shame, Laura,' Ma said, 'Anna's little and she's company. You are too big to play with dolls, anyway. Let Anna have her.'

Laura had to mind Ma. She stood at the window and saw Anna skipping down the knoll, swinging Charlotte by one arm.

'For shame, Laura,' Ma said again. 'A great girl like you, sulking about a rag doll. Stop it, this minute. You don't want that doll, you hardly ever played with it. You must not be so selfish.'

Laura quietly climbed the ladder and sat down on her box by the window. She did not cry, but she felt crying inside her because Charlotte was gone. Pa was not there, and Charlotte's box was empty. The wind went howling by the eaves. Everything was empty and cold.

'I'm sorry, Laura,' Ma said that night. 'I wouldn't have given your doll away if I'd known you care so much. But we must not think only of ourselves. Think how happy you've made Anna.'

Next morning Mr Nelson came driving up with a load of Pa's wood that he had cut. He worked all day, chopping wood for Ma, and the woodpile was big again.

'You see how good Mr Nelson is to us,' said Ma. 'The Nelsons are real good neighbours. Now aren't you glad you gave Anna your doll?'

'No, Ma,' said Laura. Her heart was crying all the time for Pa and for Charlotte.

Cold rains fell again, and froze. No more letters came from Pa. Ma thought he must have started to come home. In the night Laura listened to the wind and wondered where Pa was. Often in the mornings the woodpile was full of driven snow, and still Pa did not come. Every Saturday afternoon Laura put on her stockings and shoes, wrapped herself in Ma's big shawl, and went to the Nelsons'.

She knocked and asked if Mr Nelson had got a letter for Ma. She would not go in, she did not want to see Charlotte there. Mrs Nelson said that no letter had come, and Laura thanked her and went home.

One stormy day she caught sight of something in the Nelsons' barnyard. She stood still and looked. It was Charlotte, drowned and frozen in a puddle. Anna had thrown Charlotte away.

Laura could hardly go on to the door. She could hardly speak to Mrs Nelson. Mrs Nelson said the weather was so bad that Mr Nelson had not gone to town, but he would surely go next week. Laura said, 'Thank you, ma'am,' and turned away.

Sleety rain was beating down on Charlotte. Anna had scalped her. Charlotte's beautiful wavy hair was ripped loose, and her smiling yarn mouth was torn and bleeding red on her cheek. One shoe-button eye was gone. But she was Charlotte.

Laura snatched her up and hid her under the shawl. She ran panting against the angry wind and the sleet, all the way home. Ma started up, frightened, when she saw Laura.

'What is it! What is it? Tell me!' Ma said.

'Mr Nelson didn't go to town,' Laura answered. 'But, oh, Ma – look.'

'What on earth?' said Ma.

'It's Charlotte,' Laura said. 'I – I stole her. I don't care, Ma, I don't care if I did!'

'There, there, don't be so excited,' said Ma. 'Come here and tell me all about it,' and she drew Laura down on her lap in the rocking chair.

They decided that it had not been wrong for Laura to take back Charlotte. It had been a terrible experience for Charlotte, but Laura had rescued her and Ma promised to make her as good as new.

Ma ripped off her torn hair and the bits of her mouth and her remaining eye and her face. They thawed Charlotte and wrung her out, and Ma washed

her thoroughly clean and starched and ironed her while Laura chose from the scrap-bag a new, pale pink face for her and new button eyes.

That night when Laura went to bed she laid Charlotte in her box. Charlotte was clean and crisp, her red mouth smiled, her eyes shone black, and she had golden-brown yarn hair braided in two wee braids and tied with blue yarn bows.

Laura went to sleep cuddled against Mary under the patchwork comforters. The wind was howling and sleety rain beat on the roof. It was so cold that Laura and Mary pulled the comforters over their heads.

A terrific crash woke them. They were scared in the dark under the comforters. Then they heard a loud voice downstairs. It said,

'I declare! I dropped that armful of wood, didn't I?'

Ma was laughing, 'You did that on purpose, Charles, to wake up the girls.'

Laura flew screaming out of bed and screaming down the ladder. She jumped into Pa's arms, and so did Mary. Then what a racket of talking, laughing, jumping up and down!

Pa's blue eyes twinkled. His hair stood straight up. He was wearing new, whole boots. He had walked two hundred miles from eastern Minnesota. He had walked from town in the night, in the storm. Now he was here!

'For shame, girls, in your nightgowns!' said Ma. 'Go dress yourselves. Breakfast is almost ready.'

They dressed faster than ever before. They tumbled down the ladder and hugged Pa, and washed their hands and faces and hugged Pa, and smoothed their hair and hugged him. Jack waggled in circles and Carrie pounded the table with her spoon and sang, 'Pa's come home! Pa's come home!'

At last they were all at the table. Pa said he had been too busy, towards the last, to write. He said, 'They kept us humping on that thresher from before dawn till after dark. And when I could start home, I didn't stop to write. I didn't bring any presents, either, but I've got money to buy them.'

'The best present you could bring us, Charles, was coming home,' Ma told him.

After breakfast Pa went to see the stock. They all went with him and Jack stayed close at his heels. Pa was pleased that Sam and David and Spot looked so well. He said he couldn't have taken better care of everything, himself. Ma told him that Mary and Laura had been a great help to her.

'Gosh!' Pa said. 'It's good to be home.' Then he asked, 'What's the matter with your feet, Laura?'

She had forgotten her feet. She could walk without limping when she remembered to. She said, 'My shoes hurt, Pa.'

In the house, Pa sat down and took Carrie on his knee. Then he reached down and felt Laura's shoes.

'Ouch! My toes are tight!' Laura exclaimed.

'I should say they are!' said Pa. 'Your feet have grown since last winter. How are yours, Mary?'

Mary said her toes were tight, too.

'Take off your shoes, Mary,' said Pa. 'And Laura, you put them on.'

Mary's shoes did not pinch Laura's feet. They were good shoes, without one rip or hole in them.

'They will look almost like new when I have greased them well,' said Pa. 'Mary must have new shoes. Laura can wear Mary's, and Laura's shoes can wait for Carrie to grow to them. It won't take her long. Now what else is lacking, Caroline? Think what we need, and we'll get what we can of it. Just as soon as I can hitch up we're all going to town!'

30
Going to Town

How they hurried and scurried then! They dressed in their winter best, bundled up in coats and shawls, and climbed into the wagon. The sun shone bright and the frosty air nipped their noses. Sleet sparkled on the frozen-hard ground.

Pa was on the wagon seat, with Ma and Carrie snug beside him. Laura and Mary wrapped their shawls around each other and snuggled together on their blanket in the bottom of the wagon. Jack sat on the doorstep and watched them go; he knew they would come back soon.

Even Sam and David seemed to know that everything was all right, now that Pa was home again. They trotted gaily, till Pa said, 'Whoa!' and hitched them to the hitching-posts in front of Mr Fitch's store.

First, Pa paid Mr Fitch part of the money he owed Mr Fitch for the boards that built the house. Then, he paid for the flour and sugar that Mr Nelson had brought to Ma while Pa was gone. Next, Pa counted the money that was left, and he and Ma bought Mary's shoes.

The shoes were so new and shining on Mary's feet that Laura felt it was not fair that Mary was the oldest. Mary's shoes would always fit Laura, and Laura would never have new shoes. Then Ma said, 'Now, a dress for Laura.'

Laura hurried to Ma at the counter. Mr Fitch was taking down bolts of beautiful woollen cloth.

The winter before, Ma had let out every tuck and seam in Laura's winter dress. This winter it was very short, and there were holes in the sleeves where Laura's elbows had gone through them because they were so tight. Ma had patched them neatly, and the patches did not show, but in that dress Laura felt skimpy and patched. Still, she had not dreamed of a whole new dress.

'What do you think of this golden-brown flannel, Laura?' Ma asked.

Laura could not speak. Mr Fitch said, 'I guarantee it will wear well.'

Ma laid some narrow red braid across the golden-brown, saying, 'I think three rows of this braid, around the neckband and the cuffs and the waistband. What do you think, Laura? Would that be pretty?'

'Oh yes, Ma!' Laura said. She looked up, and her eyes and Pa's bright blue eyes danced together.

'Get it, Caroline,' said Pa. Mr Fitch measured off the

beautiful golden-brown flannel and the red braid.

Then Mary must have a new dress, but she did not like anything there. So they all crossed the street to Mr Oleson's store. There they found dark blue flannel and narrow gilt braid, which was just what Mary wanted.

Mary and Laura were admiring it while Mr Oleson measured, when Nellie Oleson came in. She was wearing a little fur shoulder cape.

'Hello!' she said, and she sniffed at the blue flannel. She said it was all right for country folks. Then she turned to show off her fur, and said, 'See what *I* got!'

They looked at it, and Nellie asked, 'Don't you wish you had a fur cape, Laura? But your Pa couldn't buy you one. Your Pa's not a storekeeper.'

Laura dared not slap Nellie. She was so angry that she could not speak. She did turn her back, and Nellie went away laughing.

Ma was buying warm cloth to make a cloak for Carrie. Pa was buying navy beans and flour and cornmeal and salt and sugar and tea. Then he must get the kerosene-can filled, and stop at the post-office. It was after noon, and growing colder, before they left town, so Pa hurried Sam and David and they trotted swiftly all the way home.

After the dinner dishes were washed and put away,

Ma opened the bundles and they all enjoyed looking their fill at the pretty dressgoods.

'I'll make your dresses as quickly as I can, girls,' said Ma. 'Because now that Pa is home we'll all be going to Sunday-school again.'

'Where's that grey challis you got for yourself, Caroline?' Pa asked her. Ma flushed pink and her head bowed while Pa looked at her. 'You mean to say you didn't get it?' he said.

Ma flashed at him. 'What about that new overcoat for yourself, Charles?'

Pa looked uncomfortable. 'I know, Caroline,' he said. 'But there won't be any crops next year when those grasshopper eggs hatch, and it's a long time till I can maybe get some work, next harvest. My old coat is good enough.'

'That's just what I thought,' said Ma, smiling at him.

After supper, when night and lamplight came, Pa took his fiddle out of the box and tuned it lovingly.

'I have missed this,' he said, looking around at them all. Then he began to play. He played 'When Johnnie Comes Marching Home.' He played 'The sweet little girl, the pretty little girl, the girl I left behind me!' He played and sang 'My Old Kentucky Home' and 'Swanee River.' Then he played and they all sang with him,

GOING TO TOWN

"Mid pleasures and palaces though we may
   roam,
Be it ever so humble, there's no place like
   home.'

31

Surprise

That was another mild winter without much snow. It was still grasshopper weather. But chill winds blew, the sky was grey, and the best place for little girls was in the cosy house.

Pa was gone outdoors all day. He hauled logs and chopped them into wood for the stove. He followed frozen Plum Creek far upstream where nobody lived, and set traps along the banks for muskrat and otter and mink.

Every morning Laura and Mary studied their books and worked sums on the slate. Every afternoon Ma heard their lessons. She said they were good little scholars, and she was sure that when they went to school again they would find they had kept up with their classes.

Every Sunday they went to Sunday-school. Laura saw Nellie Oleson showing off her fur cape. She remembered what Nellie had said about Pa, and she burned hot inside. She knew that hot feeling was wicked. She knew she must forgive Nellie, or she would never be an angel. She thought hard about the pictures of beautiful angels in the big paper-covered Bible at home. But they wore long white nightgowns. Not one of them wore a fur cape.

One happy Sunday was the Sunday when the Reverend Alden came from eastern Minnesota to preach in this Western church. He preached for a long time, while Laura looked at his soft blue eyes and watched his beard wagging. She hoped he would speak to her after church. And he did.

'Here are my little country girls, Mary and Laura!' he said. He remembered their names.

Laura was wearing her new dress that day. The skirt was long enough, and the sleeves were long, too. They made her coat sleeves look shorter than ever, but the red braid on the cuffs was pretty.

'What a pretty new dress, Laura!' the Reverend Alden said.

Laura almost forgave Nellie Oleson that day. Then came Sundays when the Reverend Alden stayed at his own far church and in Sunday-school Nellie Oleson turned up her nose at Laura and flounced her shoulders under the fur cape. Hot wickedness boiled up in Laura again.

One afternoon Ma said there would be no lessons, because they must all get ready to go to town that night. Laura and Mary were astonished.

'But we never go to town at night!' Mary said.

'There must always be a first time,' said Ma.

'But why must there be, Ma?' Laura asked. 'Why are we going to town at night?'

'It's a surprise,' said Ma. 'Now, no more questions. We must all take baths, and be our very nicest.'

In the middle of the week, Ma brought in the washtub and heated water for Mary's bath. Then again for Laura's bath, and again for Carrie's. There had never been such scrubbing and scampering, such a changing to fresh drawers and petticoats, such brushing of shoes and braiding of hair and tying on of hair ribbons. There had never been such a wondering.

Supper was early. After supper, Pa bathed in the bedroom. Laura and Mary put on their new dresses. They knew better than to ask any more questions, but they wondered and whispered together.

The wagon box was full of clean hay. Pa put Mary and Laura in it and wrapped blankets around them. He climbed to the seat beside Ma and drove away towards town.

The stars were small and frosty in the dark sky. The horses' feet clippety-clopped and the wagon rattled over the hard ground.

Pa heard something else. 'Whoa!' he said, pulling up the reins. Sam and David stopped. There was nothing but vast, dark coldness and stillness pricked by the stars. Then the stillness blossomed into the loveliest sound.

Two clear notes sounded, and sounded again and again.

No one moved. Only Sam and David tinkled their bits together and breathed. Those two notes went on, full and loud, soft and low. They seemed to be the stars singing.

Too soon Ma murmured, 'We'd better be getting on, Charles,' and the wagon rattled on. Still through its rattling Laura could hear those swaying notes.

'Oh, Pa, what is it?' she asked, and Pa said, 'It's the new church bell, Laura.'

It was for this that Pa had worn his old patched boots.

The town seemed asleep. The stores were dark as Pa drove past them. Then Laura exclaimed, 'Oh, look at the church! How pretty the church is!'

The church was full of light. Light spilled out of all its windows and ran out into the darkness from the door when it opened to let someone in. Laura almost jumped out from under the blankets before she remembered that she must never stand up in the wagon when the horses were going.

Pa drove to the church steps and helped them all out. He told them to go in, but they waited in the cold until he had covered Sam and David with their blankets. Then he came, and they all went into the church together.

Laura's mouth fell open and her eyes stretched to look

at what she saw. She held Mary's hand tightly and they followed Ma and Pa. They sat down. Then Laura could look with all her might.

Standing in front of the crowded benches was a tree. Laura decided it must be a tree. She could see its trunk and branches. But she had never before seen such a tree.

Where leaves would be in summer, there were clusters and streamers of thin green paper. Thick among them hung little sacks made of pink mosquito-bar. Laura was almost sure that she could see candy in them. From the branches hung packages wrapped in coloured paper, red packages and pink packages and yellow packages, all tied with coloured string. Silk scarves were draped among them. Red mittens hung by the cord that would go around your neck and keep them from being lost if you were wearing them. A pair of new shoes hung by their heels from a branch. Lavish strings of white popcorn were looped over all this.

Under the tree and leaning against it were all kinds of things. Laura saw a crinkly-bright washboard, a wooden tub, a churn and dasher, a sled made of new boards, a shovel, a long-handled pitchfork.

Laura was too excited to speak. She squeezed Mary's hand tighter and tighter, and she looked up at Ma, wanting so much to know what that was. Ma smiled down at her

and answered. 'That is a Christmas tree, girls. Do you think it is pretty?'

They could not answer. They nodded while they kept on looking at the wonderful tree. They were hardly even surprised to know that this was Christmas, though they had not expected Christmas yet because there was not enough snow. Just then Laura saw the most wonderful thing of all. From a far branch of that tree hung a little fur cape, and a muff to match!

The Reverend Alden was there. He preached about Christmas, but Laura was looking at that tree and she could not hear what he said. Everyone stood up to sing and Laura stood up, but she could not sing. Not a sound would come out of her throat. In the whole world, there couldn't be a store so wonderful to look at as that tree.

After the singing, Mr Tower and Mr Beadle began taking things off it, and reading out names. Mrs Tower and Miss Beadle brought those things down past the benches, and gave them to the person whose name was on them.

Everything on that tree was a Christmas present for somebody!

When Laura knew that, the lamps and people and voices and even the tree began to whirl. They whirled faster, noisier, and more excited. Someone gave her a pink mosquito-bar bag. It did have candy in it, and a big popcorn ball. Mary had one, too. So did Carrie. Every girl and boy had one. Then Mary had a pair of blue mittens. Then Laura had a red pair.

Ma opened a big package, and there was a warm, big, brown-and-red plaid shawl for her. Pa got a woolly muffler. Then Carrie had a rag doll with a china head. She screamed for joy. Through the laughing and talking and rustling of papers Mr Beadle and Mr Tower went on shouting names.

The little fur cape and muff still hung on the tree, and Laura wanted them. She wanted to look at them as long as she could. She wanted to know who got them. They could not be for Nellie Oleson who already had a fur cape.

Laura did not expect anything more. But to Mary came a pretty little booklet with Bible pictures in it, from Mrs Tower.

Mr Tower was taking the little fur cape and the muff from the tree. He read a name, but Laura could not hear it through all the joyful noise. She lost sight of the cape and muff among all the people. They were gone now.

Then to Carrie came a cunning little brown-spotted white china dog. But Carrie's arms and her eyes were full of her doll. So Laura held and stroked and laughed over the sleek little dog.

'Merry Christmas, Laura!' Miss Beadle said, and in Laura's hand she put a beautiful little box. It was made of snow-white, gleaming china. On its top stood a wee, gold-coloured tea pot and a gold-coloured tiny cup in a gold-coloured saucer.

The top of the box lifted off. Inside was a nice place to keep a breast-pin, if some day Laura had a breast-pin. Ma said it was a jewel-box.

There had never been such a Christmas as this. It was such a large, rich Christmas, the whole church full of Christmas. There were so many lamps, so many people, so much noise and laughter, and so many happinesses in it. Laura felt full and bursting, as if that whole big rich Christmas were inside her, and her mittens and her beautiful jewel-box with the wee gold cup-and-saucer and tea pot, and her candy and her popcorn ball. And suddenly someone said, 'These are for you, Laura.'

Mrs Tower stood smiling, holding out the little fur cape and muff.

'For me?' Laura said. 'For me?' Then everything else vanished while with both arms she hugged the soft furs.

She hugged them tighter and tighter, trying to believe they were really hers, that silky-soft little brown fur cape and the muff.

All around her Christmas went on, but Laura knew

only the softness of those furs. People were going home. Carrie was standing on the bench while Ma fastened her coat and tied her hood more snugly. Ma was saying, 'Thank you so much for the shawl, Brother Alden. It is just what I needed.'

Pa said, 'And I thank you for the muffler. It will feel good when I come to town in the cold.'

The Reverend Alden sat down on the bench and asked, 'And does Mary's coat fit?'

Laura had not noticed Mary's coat until then. Mary had on a new dark-blue coat. It was long, and its sleeves came to Mary's wrists. Mary buttoned it up, and it fitted.

'And how does this little girl like her furs?' the Reverend Alden smiled. He drew Laura between his knees. He laid the fur cape around her shoulders and fastened it at the throat. He put the cord of the muff around her neck, and her hands went inside the silky muff.

'There!' the Reverend Alden said. 'Now my little country girls will be warm when they come to Sunday-school.'

'What do you say, Laura?' Ma asked, but the Reverend Alden said, 'There is no need. The way her eyes are shining is enough.'

Laura could not speak. The golden-brown fur cuddled her neck and softly hugged her shoulders. Down her front it hid the threadbare fastenings of her coat. The muff came far up her wrists and hid the shortness of her coat sleeves.

'She's a little brown bird with red trimmings,' the Reverend Alden said.

Then Laura laughed. It was true. Her hair and her coat, her dress and the wonderful furs, were brown. Her hood and mittens and the braid on her dress were red.

'I'll tell my church people back East about our little brown bird,' said the Reverend Alden. 'You see, when I told them about our church out here, they said they must send a box for the Christmas tree. They all gave things they had. The little girls who sent your furs and Mary's coat needed larger ones.'

'Thank you, sir,' said Laura. 'And please, sir, tell them thank you, too.' For when she could speak, her manners were as nice as Mary's.

Then they all said good night and Merry Christmas to the Reverend Alden. Mary was so beautiful in her Christmas coat. Carrie was so pretty on Pa's arm. Pa and Ma were smiling so happily, and Laura was all gladness.

Mr and Mrs Oleson were going home, too. Mr Oleson's arms were full of things, and so were Nellie's and Willie's. No wickedness boiled up in Laura now; she only felt a little bit of mean gladness.

'Merry Christmas, Nellie,' Laura said. Nellie stared,

while Laura walked quietly on, with her hands snuggled deep in the soft muff. Her cape was prettier than Nellie's, and Nellie had no muff.

32

Grasshoppers Walking

After Christmas there were a few snowy Sundays but Pa made a bobsled of split willows and they all went to Sunday-school, snug in the new coat and the furs, the shawl and muffler.

One morning Pa said the chinook was blowing. The chinook was a warm wind from the north-west. In a day it melted the snow away, and Plum Creek was running full. Then came rains, pouring day and night. Plum Creek roared humping down its middle and swirled far beyond its low banks.

Then the air was mild, and the creek was tame again. Suddenly the plums and the willows blossomed and their new leaves uncurled. The prairies were green with grass, and Mary and Laura and Carrie ran barefooted over the fresh softness.

Every day was warmer than the day before, till hot summer came. It was time for Laura and Mary to go to school, but they did not go that year, because Pa must go away again and Ma wanted them at home with her.

The summer was very hot. Dry, hot winds blew and there was no rain.

One day when Pa came in to dinner he said, 'The grasshoppers are hatching. This hot sun is bringing them out of the eggs and up through the ground like corn popping.'

Laura ran out to see. The grass on the knoll was hopping full of tiny green things. Laura caught one in her hands and looked at it. Its wee, small wings and its tiny legs and its little head and even its eyes were the colour of the grass. It was so very tiny and so perfect. Laura could hardly believe it would ever be a big, brown, ugly grasshopper.

'They'll be big, fast enough,' said Pa. 'Eating every growing thing.'

Day by day more and more grasshoppers hatched out of the ground. Green grasshoppers of all sizes were swarming everywhere and eating. The wind could not blow loud enough to hide the sound of their jaws, nipping, gnawing, chewing.

They ate all the green garden rows. They ate the green potato tops. They ate the grass, and the willow leaves, and the green plum thickets and the small green plums. They ate the whole prairie bare and brown. And they grew.

They grew large and brown and ugly. Their big eyes bulged and their horny legs took them hopping everywhere. Thick over all the ground they were hopping, and Laura and Mary stayed in the house.

There was no rain, and the days went by hotter and hotter, uglier and uglier and filled with the sound of grasshoppers until it seemed more than could be borne.

'Oh, Charles,' Ma said one morning, 'seems to me I just can't bear one more day of this.'

Ma was sick. Her face was white and thin, and she sat down tired as she spoke.

Pa did not answer. For days he had been going out and coming in with a still, tight face. He did not sing or whistle any more. It was worst of all when he did not answer Ma. He walked to the door and stood looking out.

Even Carrie was still. They could feel the heat of the day beginning, and hear the grasshoppers. But the grasshoppers were making a new sound. Laura ran to look out at them, excited, and Pa was excited, too.

'Caroline!' he said. 'Here's a strange thing. Come look!'

All across the dooryard the grasshoppers were walking shoulder to shoulder and end to end, so crowded that the ground seemed to be moving. Not a single one hopped. Not one turned its head. As fast as they could go, they were all walking west.

Ma stood beside Pa, looking. Mary asked, 'Oh, Pa, what does it mean?' and Pa said, 'I don't know.'

He shaded his eyes and looked far to west and east. 'It's the same, as far as the eye can see. The whole ground is crawling, crawling west.'

Ma whispered, 'Oh, if they would all go away!'

They all stood looking at the strange sight. Only Carrie climbed on to her high chair and beat the table with her spoon.

'In a minute, Carrie,' Ma said. She kept on watching the grasshoppers walking by. There was no space between them and no end to them.

'I want my breakfast!' Carrie shouted. No one else moved. Finally Carrie shouted, almost crying, 'Ma! Ma!'

'There, you shall have your breakfast,' Ma said, turning around. Then she cried out, 'My goodness!'

Grasshoppers were walking over Carrie. They came pouring in the eastern window, side by side and end to end, across the window sill and down the wall and over the floor. They went up the legs of the table and the benches and Carrie's high stool. Under the table and benches, and over the table and benches and Carrie, they were walking west.

'Shut the window!' said Ma.

Laura ran on the grasshoppers to shut it. Pa went

outdoors and around the house. He came in and said, 'Better shut the upstairs windows. Grasshoppers are as thick walking up the east side of the house as they are on the ground, and they are not going around the attic window. They are going right in.'

All up the wall and across the roof went the sound of their raspy claws crawling. The house seemed full of them. Ma and Laura swept them up and threw them out the western window. None came in from the west, though the whole western side of the house was covered with grasshoppers that had walked over the roof and were walking down to the ground and going on west with the others.

That whole day long the grasshoppers walked west. All the next day they went on walking west. And all the third day they walked without stopping.

No grasshopper turned out of its way for anything.

They walked steadily over the house. They walked over the stable. They walked over Spot until Pa shut her in the stable. They walked into Plum Creek and drowned, and those behind kept on walking in and drowning until dead grasshoppers choked the creek and filled the water and live grasshoppers walked across on them.

All day the sun beat hot on the house. All day it was full of the crawling sound that went up the wall and over the roof and down. All day grasshoppers' heads with bulging eyes, and grasshoppers' legs clutching, were thick along the bottom edge of the shut windows; all day they tried to walk up the sleek glass and fell back, while thousands more pushed up and tried and fell.

Ma was pale and tight. Pa did not talk and his eyes could not twinkle. Laura could not shake the crawling sound out of her ears nor brush it off her skin.

The fourth day came and the grasshoppers went on walking. The sun shone hotter than ever, with a terribly bright light.

It was nearly noon when Pa came from the stable shouting: 'Caroline! Caroline! Look outdoors! The grasshoppers are flying!'

Laura and Mary ran to the door. Everywhere grasshoppers were spreading their wings and rising from the ground. More and more of them filled the air, flying higher and higher, till the sunshine dimmed and darkened and went out as it had done when the grasshoppers came.

Laura ran outdoors. She looked straight up at the sun through a cloud that seemed almost like snowflakes. It was a dark cloud, gleaming, glittering, shimmering bright and whiter as she looked higher and farther into it. And it was rising instead of falling.

The cloud passed over the sun and went on west until it could be seen no longer.

There was not a grasshopper left in the air or on the ground, except here and there a crippled one that could not fly but still hobbled westward.

The stillness was like the stillness after a storm.

Ma went into the house and threw herself down in the rocking-chair. 'My Lord!' she said. 'My Lord!' The words were praying, but they sounded like, 'Thank you!'

Laura and Mary sat on the doorstep. They could sit on the doorstep now; there were no grasshoppers.

'How still it is!' Mary said.

Pa leaned in the doorway and said, earnestly, 'I would like some one to tell me how they all knew at once that it was time to go, and how they knew which way was west and their ancestral home.'

But no one could tell him.

33

Wheels of Fire

All the days were peaceful after that July day when the grasshoppers flew away.

Rain fell and grass grew again over all the land that they had eaten bare and left brown and ugly. Ragweeds grew faster, and careless weeds, and the big, spreading tumbleweeds like bushes.

Willows and cottonwoods and plum thickets put out leaves again. There would be no fruit, for blossom-time was past. There would be no wheat. But wild hay was growing coarse in low places by the creek. Potatoes lived, and there were fish in the fish-trap.

Pa hitched Sam and David to Mr Nelson's plough, and ploughed part of the weedy wheat-field. He ploughed a wide fire-break west of the house, from the creek to the creek again. On the field he sowed turnip seeds.

'It's late,' he said. 'The old folks say to sow turnips the twenty-fifth of July, wet or dry. But I guess the old folks didn't figure on grasshoppers. And likely there will be as many turnips as you and the girls can handle, Caroline. I won't be here to do it.'

He must go away to the east again, to work where there were harvests, for the house was not yet paid for and he must buy salt and cornmeal and sugar. He could not stay to cut the hay that Sam and David and Spot must have to eat next winter. But Mr Nelson agreed to cut and stack Pa's wild hay for a share of it.

Then one early morning Pa went walking away. He went whistling out of sight, with his jumper-roll on his shoulder. But there was not one hole in his boots. He would not mind the walk, and some day he would come walking back again.

In the mornings after the chores and the housework were done, Laura and Mary studied their books. In the afternoons Ma heard their lessons. Then they might play or sew their seams, till time to meet the herd and bring Spot and her calf home. Then came chores again and supper and the supper dishes and bedtime.

After Mr Nelson stacked Pa's hay by the stable, the days were warm on the sunny side of the stacks, but their shady sides were cool. The wind blew chill and the mornings were frosty.

One morning when Laura drove Spot and her calf to meet the herd, Johnny was having trouble with the cattle. He was trying to drive them out on the prairie to the west, where the frostbitten, brown grass was tall. The cattle did not want to go. They kept turning and dodging back.

Laura and Jack helped him drive them. The sun was coming up then and the sky was clear. But before Laura got back to the house, she saw a low cloud in the west. She wrinkled her nose and sniffed long and deep, and she remembered Indian Territory.

'Ma!' she called. Ma came outdoors and looked at the cloud.

'It's far away, Laura,' Ma said. 'Likely it won't come so far.'

All morning the wind blew out of the west. At noon it was blowing more strongly, and Ma and Mary and Laura stood in the dooryard and watched the dark cloud coming nearer.

'I wonder where the herd is,' Ma worried.

At last they could see a flickering brightness under the cloud.

'If the cows are safe across the creek we needn't worry,' said Ma. 'Fire can't cross that fire-break. Better come in the house, girls, and eat your dinner.'

She took Carrie into the house, but Laura and Mary looked just once more at the smoke rolling nearer. Then Mary pointed and opened her mouth but could not speak. Laura screamed, 'Ma! Ma! A wheel of fire!'

In front of the red-flickering smoke a wheel of fire came

rolling swiftly, setting fire to the grass as it came. Another and another, another, came rolling fast before the wind. The first one was whirling across the fire-break.

With water-pail and mop Ma ran to meet it. She struck it with the wet mop and beat it out black on the ground. She ran to meet the next one, but more and more were coming.

'Stay back, Laura!' she said.

Laura stayed backed flat against the house, holding Mary's hand tight, and watching. In the house Carrie was crying because Ma had shut her in.

The wheels of fire came on, faster and faster. They were the big tumbleweeds, that had ripened round and dry and pulled up their small roots so that the wind would blow them far and scatter their seeds. Now they were burning, but still they rolled before the roaring wind and the roaring big fire that followed them.

Smoke swirled now around Ma where she ran, beating with her mop at those fiery swift wheels. Jack shivered against Laura's legs and tears ran out of her smarting eyes.

Mr Nelson's grey colt came galloping and Mr Nelson jumped off it at the stable. He grabbed a pitchfork and shouted: 'Run quick! Bring wet rags!' He went running to help Ma.

Laura and Mary ran to the creek with gunny sacks.

They ran back with them sopping wet and Mr Nelson put one on the pitchfork tines. Ma's pail was empty; they ran and filled it.

The wheels of fire were running up the knoll. Streaks of fire followed through the dry grass. Ma and Mr Nelson fought them with the mop and the wet sacks.

'The hay-stacks! The hay-stacks!' Laura screamed. One wheel of fire had got to the hay-stacks. Mr Nelson and Ma went running through the smoke. Another wheel came rolling over the black-burned ground to the house. Laura was so frightened that she did not know what she was doing. Carrie was in the house. Laura beat that burning wheel to death with a wet gunny sack.

Then there were no more wheels. Ma and Mr Nelson had stopped the fire at the hay-stack. Bits of sooty hay and grass swirled in the air, while the big fire rushed to the fire-break.

It could not get across. It ran fast to the south, to the creek. It ran north and came to the creek there. It could not go any farther, so it dwindled down and died where it was.

The clouds of smoke were blowing away and the prairie fire was over. Mr Nelson said he had gone on his grey colt after the cattle; they were safe on the other side of the creek.

'We are grateful to you, Mr Nelson,' said Ma. 'You saved our place. The girls and I could never have done it alone.'

When he had gone away she said, 'There is nothing in the world so good as good neighbours. Come now, girls, and wash, and eat your dinner.'

34

Marks on the Slate

After the prairie fire the weather was so cold that Ma said they must hurry to dig the potatoes and pull the turnips before they froze.

She dug the potatoes while Mary and Laura picked them up and carried them down to the cellar in pails. The wind blew hard and sharp. They wore their shawls, but of course not their mittens. Mary's nose was red and Laura's was icy cold, and their hands were stiff and their feet were numb. But they were glad they had so many potatoes.

It was good to thaw by the stove when the chores were done, and to smell the warm smells of potatoes boiling and fish frying. It was good to eat and to go to bed.

Then in dark, gloomy weather they pulled the turnips. That was harder than picking up potatoes. The turnips were big and stubborn, and often Laura pulled till she sat down hard when the turnip came up.

All the juicy green tops must be cut off with the butcher knife. The juice wet their hands and the wind chapped them till they cracked and bled, and Ma made a salve of lard and bees-wax melted together, to rub on their hands at night.

But Spot and her calf ate the juicy turnip tops and saved them. And it was good to know that there were turnips enough in the cellar to last all winter long. There would be boiled turnips, and mashed turnips and creamed turnips. And in the winter evenings a plate of raw turnips would be on the table by the lamp; they would peel off the thick rinds and eat the raw turnips in crisp, juicy slices.

One day they put the last turnip in the cellar, and Ma said, 'Well, it can freeze now.'

Sure enough, that night the ground froze, and in the morning snow was falling thick outside the windows.

Now Mary thought of a way to count the days until Pa would come home. His last letter had said that two more weeks would finish the threshing where he was. Mary brought out the slate, and on it she made a mark for each day of one week, seven marks. Under them she made another mark for each day of the next week, seven more marks.

The last mark was for the day he would come. But when they showed the slate to Ma, she said, 'Better make marks for another week, for Pa to walk home on.'

So Mary slowly made seven marks more. Laura did not like to see so many marks between now and the time that Pa would come home. But every night before they went to bed, Mary rubbed out one mark. That was one day gone.

Every morning Laura thought, 'This whole day must go by before Mary can rub out another mark.'

Outdoors smelled good in the chilly mornings. The sun had melted away the snow, but the ground was hard and frosty. Plum Creek was still awake. Brown leaves were floating away on the water under the wintry blue sky.

At night it was cosy to be in the lamplit house by the warm stove. Laura played with Carrie and Jack on the clean, smooth floor. Ma sat comfortably mending, and Mary's book was spread under the lamp.

'It's bedtime, girls,' Ma said, taking off her thimble. Then Mary rubbed out one more mark, and put the slate away.

One night she rubbed out the first day of the last week. They all watched her do it, and Mary said, as she put the slate away, 'Pa is walking home now! Those are the marks he will walk on.'

In the corner Jack suddenly made a glad sound, as if he understood her. He ran to the door. He stood up against the door, scratching and whining and waggling. Then Laura heard, faintly whistling through the wind, 'When Johnny Comes Marching Home.'

'It's Pa! Pa!' she shrieked and tore the door open and ran pell-mell down through the windy dark with Jack bounding ahead.

'Hullo, half-pint!' Pa said, hugging her tight. 'Good dog, Jack!' Lamplight streamed from the door and Mary was coming, and Ma and Carrie. 'How's my little one?' Pa said, giving Carrie a toss. 'Here's my big girl,' and he pulled Mary's braid. 'Give me a kiss, Caroline, if you can reach me through these wild Indians.'

Then there was supper to get for Pa, and no one thought of going to bed. Laura and Mary told him everything at once, about the wheels of fire and potatoes and turnips and how big Spot's calf was and how far they had studied in their books, and Mary said: 'But, Pa, you can't be here. You didn't walk off the marks on the slate.'

She showed him the marks still there, the marks he was to walk on.

'I see!' said Pa. 'But you did not rub out the marks for the days it took my letter to come so far. I hurried fast all the way, too, for they say it's already a hard winter in the north. What do we need to get in town, Caroline?'

Ma said they did not need anything. They had eaten so many fish and potatoes that the flour was still holding out, and the sugar, and even the tea. Only the salt was low, and it would last several days.

'Then I'd better get the wood up before we go to town,' said Pa. 'I don't like the sound of that wind, and they tell me that Minnesota blizzards come up fast and sudden. I heard of some folks that went to town and a blizzard came up so quickly they couldn't get back. Their children at home burned all the furniture, but they froze stark stiff before the blizzard cleared up enough so the folks could get home.'

35
Keeping House

Now in the daytimes Pa was driving the wagon up and down Plum Creek, and bringing load after load of logs to the pile by the door. He cut down old plum trees and old willows and cotton-woods, leaving the little ones to grow. He hauled them and stacked them, and chopped and split them into stove wood, till he had a big woodpile.

With his short-handled axe in his belt, his traps on his arm, and his gun against his shoulder, he walked far up Plum Creek, setting traps for muskrat and mink and otter and fox.

One evening at supper Pa said he had found a beaver meadow. But he did not set traps there because so few beavers were left. He had seen a fox and shot at it, but missed.

'I am all out of practice hunting,' he said. 'It's a fine place we have here, but there isn't much game. Makes a fellow think of places out West where –'

'Where there are no schools for the children, Charles,' said Ma.

'You're right, Caroline. You usually are,' Pa said. 'Listen to that wind. We'll have a storm tomorrow.'

But the next day was mild as spring. The air was soft and warm and the sun shone brightly. In the middle of the morning Pa came to the house.

'Let's have an early dinner and take a walk to town this afternoon,' he said to Ma. 'This is too nice a day for you to stay indoors. Time enough for that when winter really comes.'

'But the children,' said Ma. 'We can't take Carrie and walk so far.'

'Shucks!' Pa laughed at her. 'Mary and Laura are great girls now. They can take care of Carrie for one afternoon.'

'Of course we can, Ma,' said Mary; and Laura said, 'Of course we can!'

They watched Pa and Ma starting gaily away. Ma was so pretty, in her brown-and-red Christmas shawl, with her brown knit hood tied under her chin, and she stepped so quickly and looked up at Pa so merrily that Laura thought she was like a bird.

Then Laura swept the floor while Mary cleared the table. Mary washed the dishes and Laura wiped them and put them in the cupboard. They put the red-checked cloth on the table. Now the whole long afternoon was before them and they could do as they pleased.

First, they decided to play school. Mary said she must be Teacher, because she was older and besides she knew more. Laura knew that was true. So Mary was Teacher and she liked it, but Laura was soon tired of that play.

'I know,' Laura said. 'Let's both teach Carrie her letters.'

They sat Carrie on a bench and held the book before her, and both did their best. But Carrie did not like it. She would not learn the letters, so they had to stop that.

'Well,' said Laura, 'let's play keeping house.'

'We *are* keeping house,' said Mary. 'What is the use of playing it?'

The house was empty and still, with Ma gone. Ma was so quiet and gentle that she never made any noise, but now the whole house was listening for her.

Laura went outdoors for a while by herself, but she came back. The afternoon grew longer and longer. There was nothing at all to do. Even Jack walked up and down restlessly.

He asked to go out, but when Laura opened the door he would not go. He lay down and got up, and walked around and around the room. He came to Laura and looked at her earnestly.

'What is it, Jack?' Laura asked him. He stared hard at her, but she could not understand, and he almost howled.

'Don't, Jack!' Laura told him, quickly. 'You scare me.'

'Is it something outdoors?' Mary wondered. Laura ran out, but on the doorstep Jack took hold of her dress and pulled her back. Outdoors was bitter cold. Laura shut the door.

'Look,' she said. 'The sunshine's dark. Are the grasshoppers coming back?'

'Not in the winter-time, goosie,' said Mary. 'Maybe it's rain.'

'Goosie yourself!' Laura said back. 'It doesn't rain in the winter-time.'

'Well, snow, then! What's the difference?' Mary was angry and so was Laura. They would have gone on quarrelling, but suddenly there was no sunshine. They ran to look through the bedroom window.

A dark cloud with a fleecy white underside was rolling fast from the north-west.

Mary and Laura looked out of the front window. Surely it was time for Pa and Ma to come, but they were nowhere in sight.

'Maybe it's a blizzard,' said Mary.

'Like Pa told us about,' said Laura.

They looked at each other through the grey air. They were thinking of those children who froze stark stiff.

'The woodbox is empty,' said Laura.

Mary grabbed her. 'You can't!' said Mary. 'Ma told us

to stay in the house if it stormed.' Laura jerked away and Mary said, 'Besides, Jack won't let you.'

'We've got to bring in wood before the storm gets here,' Laura told her. 'Hurry!'

They could hear a strange sound in the wind, like a faraway screaming. They put on their shawls and pinned them under their chins with their large shawl-pins. They put on their mittens.

Laura was ready first. She told Jack, 'We've got to bring in wood, Jack.' He seemed to understand. He went out with her and stayed close at her heels. The wind was colder than icicles. Laura ran to the woodpile, piled up a big armful of wood, and ran back, with Jack behind her. She could not open the door while she held the wood. Mary opened it for her.

Then they did not know what to do. The cloud was coming swiftly, and they must both bring in wood before the storm got there. They could not open the door when their arms were full of wood. They could not leave the door open and let the cold come in.

'I tan open the door,' said Carrie.

'You can't,' Mary said.

'I tan, too!' said Carrie, and she reached up both hands and turned the door knob. She could do it! Carrie was big enough to open the door.

Laura and Mary hurried fast, bringing in wood. Carrie opened the door when they came to it, and shut it behind them. Mary could carry larger armfuls, but Laura was quicker.

They filled the woodbox before it began to snow. The snow came suddenly with a whirling blast, and it was small hard grains like sand. It stung Laura's face where it struck. When Carrie opened the door, it swirled into the house in a white cloud.

Laura and Mary forgot that Ma had told them to stay in the house when it stormed. They forgot everything but bringing in wood. They ran frantically back and forth, bringing each time all the wood they could stagger under.

They piled wood around the woodbox and around the stove. They piled it against the wall. They made the piles higher, and bigger.

Bang! they banged the door. They ran to the woodpile. Clop-clop-clop they stacked the wood on their arms. They ran to the door. Bump! it went open, and bang! they back-bumped it shut, and thumpity-thud-thump! they flung down the wood and ran back, outdoors, to the woodpile, and panting back again.

They could hardly see the woodpile in the swirling whiteness. Snow was driven all in among the wood. They could hardly see the house, and Jack was a dark blob

hurrying beside them. The hard snow scoured their faces. Laura's arms ached and her chest panted and all the time she thought, 'Oh, where is Pa? Where is Ma?' and she felt 'Hurry! Hurry!' and she heard the wind screeching.

The woodpile was gone. Mary took a few sticks and Laura took a few sticks and there were no more. They ran to the door together, and Laura opened it and Jack bounded in. Carrie was at the front window, clapping her hands and squealing. Laura dropped her sticks of wood and turned just in time to see Pa and Ma burst, running, out of the whirling whiteness of snow.

Pa was holding Ma's hand and pulling to help her run. They burst into the house and slammed the door and stood panting, covered with snow. No one said anything while Pa and Ma looked at Laura and Mary, who stood all snowy in shawls and mittens.

At last Mary said in a small voice, 'We did go out in the storm, Ma. We forgot.'

Laura's head bowed down and she said, 'We didn't want to burn up the furniture, Pa, and freeze stark stiff.'

'Well, I'll be darned!' said Pa. 'If they didn't move the whole woodpile in. All the wood I cut to last a couple of weeks.'

There, piled up in the house, was the whole woodpile. Melted snow was leaking out of it and spreading in puddles. A wet path went to the door, where snow lay unmelted.

Then Pa's great laugh rang out, and Ma's gentle smile shone warm on Mary and Laura. They knew they were forgiven for disobeying, because they had been wise to bring in wood, though perhaps not quite so much wood.

Sometime soon they would be old enough not to make any mistakes, and then they could always decide what to do. They would not have to obey Pa and Ma any more.

They bustled to take off Ma's shawl and hood and brush the snow from them and hang them up to dry. Pa hurried to the stable to do the chores before the storm grew worse. Then while Ma rested, they stacked the wood neatly as she told them, and they swept and mopped the floor.

The house was neat and cosy again. The tea-kettle hummed, the fire shone brightly from the draughts above the stove hearth. Snow swished against the windows.

Pa came in. 'Here is the little milk I could get here with. The wind blew it up out of the pail. Caroline, this is a terrible storm. I couldn't see an inch, and the wind comes from all directions at once. I thought I was on the path, but I couldn't see the house, and – well, I just barcly bumped against the corner. Another foot to the left and I never would have got in.'

'*Charles!*' Ma said.

'Nothing to be scared about now,' said Pa. 'But if we hadn't run all the way from town and beat this storm here –' Then his eyes twinkled, he rumpled Mary's hair and pulled Laura's ear. 'I'm glad all this wood is in the house, too,' he said.

36

Prairie Winter

Next day the storm was even worse. It could not be seen through the windows, for snow swished so thickly against them that the glass was like white glass. All around the house the wind was howling.

When Pa started to the stable, snow whirled thick into the lean-to, and outdoors was a wall of whiteness. He took down a coil of rope from a nail in the lean-to.

'I'm afraid to try it without something to guide me back,' he said. 'With this rope tied to the far end of the clothes-line I ought to reach the stable.'

They waited, frightened, till Pa came back. The wind had taken almost all the milk out of the pail, and Pa had to thaw by the stove before he could talk. He had felt his way along the clothes-line fastened to the lean-to, till he came to the clothes-line post. Then he tied an end of his rope to the post and went on, unwinding the rope from his arm as he went.

He could not see anything but the whirling snow. Suddenly something hit him, and it was the stable wall.

He felt along it till he came to the door, and there he fastened the end of the rope.

So he did the chores and came back, holding on to the rope.

All day the storm lasted. The windows were white and the wind never stopped howling and screaming. It was pleasant in the warm house. Laura and Mary did their lessons, then Pa played the fiddle while Ma rocked and knitted, and bean soup simmered on the stove.

All night the storm lasted, and all the next day. Firelight danced out of the stove's draught, and Pa told stories and played the fiddle.

Next morning the wind was only whizzing, and the sun shone. Through the window Laura saw snow scudding before the wind in fast white swirls over the ground. The whole world looked like Plum Creek foaming in flood, only the flood was snow. Even the sunshine was bitter cold.

'Well, I guess the storm is over,' said Pa. 'If I can get to town tomorrow, I am going to lay in a supply of food.'

Next day the snow was in drifts on the ground. The wind blew only a smoke of snow up the sides and off the tops of the drifts. Pa drove to town and brought back big sacks of cornmeal, flour, sugar, and beans. It was enough food to last a long time.

'Seems strange to have to figure where meat is coming from,' Pa said. 'In Wisconsin we always had plenty of bear meat and venison, and in Indian Territory there were deer and antelope, jackrabbits, turkeys, and geese, all the meat a man could want. Here there are only little cotton-tail rabbits.'

'We will have to plan ahead and raise meat,' said Ma. 'Think how easy it will be to fatten our own meat, where we can raise such fields of grain for feed.'

'Yes,' Pa said. 'Next year we will raise a wheat crop, surely.'

Next day another blizzard came. Again that low, dark cloud rolled swiftly up from the north-west till it blotted out the sun and covered the whole sky and the wind went, howling and shrieking, whirling snow until nothing could be seen but a blur of whiteness.

Pa followed the rope to the stable and back. Ma cooked and cleaned and mended and helped Mary and Laura with their lessons. They did the dishes, made their bed, and swept the floors, kept their hands and faces clean and neatly braided their hair. They studied their books and played with Carrie and Jack. They drew pictures on their slate, and taught Carrie to make her A B C's.

Mary was still sewing nine-patch blocks. Now Laura started a bear's-track quilt. It was harder than a nine-patch, because there were bias seams, very hard to make smooth. Every seam must be exactly right before Ma would let her make another, and often Laura worked several days on one short seam.

So they were busy all day long. And all the days ran together, with blizzard after blizzard. No sooner did one blizzard end with a day of cold sunshine, than another began. On the sunny day Pa worked quickly, chopping more wood, visiting his traps, pitching hay from the snowy stacks into the stable. Even though the sunny day was not Monday, Ma washed the clothes and hung them on the clothes-line to freeze dry. That day there were no lessons. Laura and Mary and Carrie, bundled stiff in thick wraps, could play outdoors in the sunshine.

Next day another blizzard came, but Pa and Ma had everything ready for it.

If the sunny day were Sunday, they could hear the church bell. Clear and sweet it rang through the cold, and they all stood outdoors and listened.

They could not go to Sunday-school; a blizzard might come before they could reach home. But every Sunday they had a little Sunday-school of their own.

Laura and Mary repeated their Bible verses. Ma read a Bible story and a psalm. Then Pa played hymns on the fiddle, and they all sang. They sang:

'When gloomy clouds across the sky
    Cast shadows o'er the land,
Bright rays of hope illume my path,
    For Jesus holds my hand.'

Every Sunday Pa played and they sang:

'Sweet Sabbath school more dear to me
    Than fairest palace dome,
My heart e'er turns with joy to thee,
    My own dear Sabbath home.'

37

The Long Blizzard

A storm was dying down at supper-time one day, and Pa said: 'Tomorrow I'm going to town. I need some tobacco for my pipe and I want to hear the news. Do you need anything, Caroline?'

'No, Charles,' said Ma. 'Don't go. These blizzards come up so fast.'

'There'll be no danger tomorrow,' said Pa. 'We've just had a three-days' blizzard. There's plenty of wood chopped to last through the next one, and I can take time to go to town now.'

'Well, if you think best,' Ma said. 'At least, Charles, promise me that you will stay in town if a storm comes up.'

'I wouldn't try to stir a step without safe hold of a rope, in one of these storms,' said Pa. 'But it is not like you, Caroline, to be afraid to have me go anywhere.'

'I can't help it,' Ma answered. 'I don't feel right about your going. I have a feeling – it's just foolishness, I guess.'

Pa laughed. 'I'll bring in the woodpile, just in case I do have to stay in town.'

He filled the woodbox and piled wood high around

it. Ma urged him to put on an extra pair of socks, to keep his feet from being frost-bitten. So Laura brought the bootjack and Pa pulled off his boots and drew another pair of socks over those he already wore. Ma gave him a new pair which she had just finished knitting of thick, warm wool.

'I do wish you had a buffalo overcoat,' said Ma. 'That old coat is worn so thin.'

'And I wish you had some diamonds,' said Pa. 'Don't you worry, Caroline. It won't be long till spring.'

Pa smiled at them while he buckled the belt of his old, threadbare overcoat and put on his warm felt cap.

'That wind is so bitter cold, Charles,' Ma worried. 'Do pull down the earflaps.'

'Not this morning!' said Pa. 'Let the wind whistle! Now you girls be good, all of you, till I come back.' And his eyes twinkled at Laura as he shut the door behind him.

After Laura and Mary had washed and wiped the dishes, swept the floor, made their bed, and dusted, they settled down with their books. But the house was so cosy and pretty that Laura kept looking up at it.

The black stove was polished till it gleamed. A kettle of beans was bubbling on its top and bread was baking in the oven. Sunshine slanted through the shining windows between the pink-edged curtains. The red-checked cloth was on the table. Beside the clock on its shelf stood Carrie's little brown-and-white dog, and Laura's sweet jewel-box. And the little pink-and-white shepherdess stood smiling on the wood-brown bracket.

Ma had brought her mending-basket to her rocking-chair by the window, and Carrie sat on the footstool by her knee. While Ma rocked and mended, she heard Carrie say her letters in the primer. Carrie told big A and little a, big B and little b, then she laughed and talked and looked at the pictures. She was still so little that she did not have to keep quiet and study.

The clock struck twelve. Laura watched its pendulum wagging, and the black hands moving on the round white face. It was time for Pa to come home. The beans were cooked, the bread was baked. Everything was ready for Pa's dinner.

Laura's eyes strayed to the window. She stared a moment before she knew that something was wrong with the sunshine.

'Ma!' she cried. 'The sun is a funny colour.'

Ma looked up from her mending, startled. She went quickly into the bedroom, where she could see the north-west, and she came quietly back.

'You may put away your books, girls,' she said. 'Bundle up and bring in more wood. If Pa hasn't started home he will stay in town and we will need more wood in the house.'

From the woodpile Laura and Mary saw the dark cloud coming. They hurried, they ran, but there was time only to get into the house with their armloads of wood before the storm came howling. It seemed angry that they had got the two loads of wood. Snow whirled so thickly that they could not see the doorstep, and Ma said:

'That will do for now. The storm can't get much worse, and Pa may come in a few minutes.'

Mary and Laura took off their wraps and warmed their cold-stiff hands. Then they waited for Pa.

The wind shrieked and howled and jeered around the house. Snow swished against the blank windows. The long black hand of the clock moved slowly around its face, the short hand moved to one, and then to two.

Ma dished up three bowls of the hot beans. She broke into pieces a small loaf of the fresh warm bread.

'Here, girls,' she said. 'You might as well eat your dinner. Pa must have stayed in town.'

She had forgotten to fill a bowl for herself. Then she forgot to eat until Mary reminded her. Even then she did not really eat; she said she was not hungry.

The storm was growing worse. The house trembled in the wind. Cold crept over the floor, and powdery snow was driven in around the windows and the doors that Pa had made so tight.

'Pa has surely stayed in town,' Ma said. 'He will stay there all night, and I'd better do the chores now.'

She drew on Pa's old, tall stable-boots. Her little feet were lost in them, but they would keep out the snow. She fastened Pa's jumper snug at her throat and belted it around her waist. She tied her hood and put on her mittens.

'May I go with you, Ma?' Laura asked.

'No,' said Ma. 'Now listen to me. Be careful of fire. Nobody but Mary is to touch the stove, no matter how long I am gone. Nobody is to go outdoors, or even open a door, till I come back.'

She hung the milk-pail on her arm, and reached through the whirling snow till she got hold of the clothes-line. She shut the back door behind her.

Laura ran to the darkened window, but she could not see Ma. She could see nothing but the whirling whiteness swishing against the glass. The wind screamed and howled and gibbered. There seemed to be voices in it.

Ma would go step by step, holding tight to the clothes-line. She would come to the post and go on, blind in the hard snow whirling and scratching her cheeks. Laura tried to think slowly, one step at a time, till now, surely, Ma bumped against the stable door.

Ma opened the door and blew in with the snow. She turned and pushed the door shut quickly, and dropped the latch into its notch. The stable would be warm from the heat of the animals, and steamy with their breath. It was quiet there; the storm was outside, and the sod walls were thick. Now Sam and David turned their heads and whickered to Ma. The cow coaxed, 'Moo-oo,' and the big calf cried, 'Baw!' The pullets were scratching here and there, and one of the hens was saying to herself, 'Crai-ai-kree-eek.'

Ma would clean all the stalls with the pitchfork. Forkful by forkful she threw the old bedding on the manure-pile. Then she took the hay they had left in their mangers, and spread it to make them clean beds.

From the hay-pile she pitched fresh hay into manger after manger, till all four mangers were full. Sam and David and Spot and her calf munched the rustling good hay. They were not very thirsty, because Pa had watered them all before he went to town.

With the old knife that Pa kept by the turnip-pile Ma cut up turnips. She put some in each feedbox, and now the horses and cattle crunched the crisp turnips. Ma looked at the hens' water-dish to make sure they had water. She scattered a little corn for them, and gave them a turnip to peck.

Now she must be milking Spot.

Laura waited until she was sure that Ma was hanging up the milking-stool. Carefully fastening the stable door behind her, Ma came back towards the house, holding tight to the rope.

But she did not come. Laura waited a long time. She made up her mind to wait longer, and she did. The wind was shaking the house now. Snow as fine and grainy as sugar covered the window sill and sifted off to the floor and did not melt.

Laura shivered in her shawl. She kept on staring at the blank window-panes, hearing the swishing snow and the howling, jeering winds. She was thinking of the children whose Pa and Ma never came. They burned all the furniture and froze stark stiff.

Then Laura could be still no longer. The fire was burning well, but only that end of the room was really warm. Laura pulled the rocking-chair near the open oven and set Carrie in it and straightened her dress. Carrie rocked the chair gaily, while Laura and Mary went on waiting.

At last the back door burst open. Laura flew to Ma. Mary took the milk-pail while Laura untied Ma's hood. Ma was too cold and breathless to speak. They helped her out of the jumper.

The first thing she said was, 'Is there any milk left?'

There was a little milk in the bottom of the pail, and some was frozen to the pail's inside.

'The wind is terrible,' Ma said. She warmed her hands, and then she lighted the lamp and set it on the window sill.

'Why are you doing that, Ma?' Mary asked her, and Ma said, 'Don't you think the lamplight's pretty, shining against the snow outside?'

When she was rested, they ate their supper of bread

and milk. Then they all sat still by the stove and listened. They heard the voices howling and shrieking in the wind, and the house creaking, and the snow swishing.

'This will never do!' said Ma. 'Let's play bean-porridge hot! Mary, you and Laura play it together, and, Carrie, you hold up your hands. We'll do it faster than Mary and Laura can!'

So they all played bean-porridge hot, faster and faster until they could not say the rhymes, for laughing. Then Mary and Laura washed the supper cups, while Ma settled down to her knitting.

Carrie wanted more bean-porridge hot, so Mary and Laura took turns playing it with her. Every time they stopped she shouted, 'More! More!'

The voices in the storm howled and giggled and shrieked, and the house trembled. Laura was patting on Carrie's hands,

> 'Some like it hot, some like it cold,
> Some like it in the pot, nine days –'

The stovepipe sharply rattled. Laura looked up and screamed, 'Ma! The house is on fire!'

A ball of fire was rolling down the stovepipe. It was bigger than Ma's big ball of yarn. It rolled across the stove and dropped to the floor as Ma sprang up. She snatched up her skirts and stamped on it. But it seemed to jump through her foot, and it rolled to the knitting she had dropped.

Ma tried to brush it into the ashpan. It ran in front of her knitting needles, but it followed the needles back. Another ball of fire had rolled down the stovepipe, and another. They rolled across the floor after the knitting needles and did not burn the floor.

'My goodness!' Ma said.

While they watched those balls of fire rolling, suddenly there were only two. Then there were none. No one had seen where they went.

'That is the strangest thing I ever saw,' said Ma. She was afraid.

All the hair on Jack's back was standing up. He walked to the door, lifted up his nose, and howled.

Mary cowered in her chair and Ma put her hands over her ears. 'For pity's sake, Jack, hush,' she begged him.

Laura ran to Jack, but he did not want to be hugged. He went back to his corner and lay with his nose on his paws, his hair bristling and his eyes shining in the shadow.

Ma held Carrie, and Laura and Mary crowded into the rocking-chair, too. They heard the wild voices of the storm and felt Jack's eyes shining, till Ma said:

'Better run along to bed, girls. The sooner you're asleep, the sooner it will be morning.'

She kissed them good night, and Mary climbed the attic ladder. But Laura stopped half-way up. Ma was warming Carrie's nightgown by the oven. Laura asked her, low, 'Pa did stay in town, didn't he?'

Ma did not look up. She said cheerfully, 'Why, surely, Laura. No doubt he and Mr Fitch are sitting by the stove now, telling stories and cracking jokes.'

Laura went on to bed. Deep in the night she woke and saw lamplight shining up through the ladder-hole. She crept out of bed into the cold, and kneeling on the floor she looked down.

Ma sat alone in her chair. Her head was bowed and she was very still, but her eyes were open, looking at her hands clasped in her lap. The lamp was shining in the window.

For a long time Laura looked down. Ma did not move. The lamp went on shining. The storm howled and hooted after things that fled shrieking through the enormous dark around the frightened house. At last Laura crept silently back to bed and lay shivering.

38
The Day of Games

It was late next morning when Ma called Laura to breakfast. The storm was fiercer and wilder. Furry-white frost covered the windows, and inside that good tight house the sugary snow was over the floor and the bedcovers. Upstairs was so cold that Laura snatched up her clothes and hurried down to dress by the stove.

Mary was already dressed and buttoning Carrie up. Hot cornmeal mush, and milk, with the new white bread and butter, were on the table. The daylight was dim white. Frost was thick on every window pane.

Ma shivered over the stove. 'Well,' she said, 'the stock must be fed.'

She put on Pa's boots and jumper, and wrapped herself in the big shawl. She told Mary and Laura that she would be gone longer this time, because she must water the horses and the cattle.

When she was gone, Mary was scared and still. But Laura could not bear to be still. 'Come on,' she told Mary. 'We've got the work to do.'

They washed and wiped the dishes. They shook the

snow off their bedcovers and made their bed. They warmed again by the stove, then they polished it, and Mary cleaned the woodbox while Laura swept the floors.

Ma had not come back. So Laura took the dust-cloth and wiped the window sills and the benches and every curve of Ma's willow rocking-chair. She climbed on a bench and very carefully wiped the clock-shelf and the clock, and the little brown-spotted dog and her own jewel-box with the gold tea pot and cup-and-saucer on top. But she did not touch the pretty china shepherdess standing on the bracket that Pa had carved for Ma. Ma allowed no one else to touch the shepherdess.

While Laura was dusting, Mary combed Carrie's hair and put the red-checked cloth on the table, and got out the school-books and the slate.

At last the wind howled into the lean-to with a cloud of snow and Ma.

Her skirt and her shawl were frozen stiff with ice. She had had to draw water from the well for the horses and Spot and the calf. The wind had flung the water on her and the cold had frozen her soaked clothes. She had not been able to get to the barn with enough water. But under the icy shawl she had saved almost all the milk.

She rested a little, and said she must bring in wood. Mary and Laura begged her to let them bring it, but Ma said:

'No. You girls are not big enough and you'd be lost. You do not know what this storm is like. I'll get the wood. You open the door for me.'

She piled wood high on the woodbox and around it, while they opened and shut the door for her. Then she rested, and they mopped up the puddles of snow melting from the wood.

'You are good girls,' Ma said. She looked around at the house, and praised them for doing the work so nicely while she was gone. 'Now,' she said, 'you may study your lessons.'

Laura and Mary sat down to their books. Laura looked steadily at the page, but she could not study. She heard the storm howling and she heard things in the air moaning and shrieking. Snow swish-swished against the windows. She tried not to think of Pa. Suddenly the words on the page smeared together and a drop of water splashed on them.

She was ashamed. It would be shameful even for Carrie to cry, and Laura was eight years old. She looked side wise to make sure that Mary had not seen that tear fall. Mary's eyes were shut so tight that her whole face was crinkled, and Mary's mouth was wobbling.

'I don't believe we want lessons, girls!' Ma said. 'Suppose we don't do anything today but play. Think what we'll play first. Pussy-in-the-corner! Would you like that?'

'Oh yes!' they said.

Laura stood in one corner. Mary in another, and Carrie in the third. There were only three corners, because the stove was in one. Ma stood in the middle of the floor and cried, 'Poor pussy wants a corner!'

Then all at once they ran out of their corners and each tried to get into another corner. Jack was excited. Ma dodged into Mary's corner, and that left Mary out to be poor pussy. Then Laura fell over Jack, and that left Laura out. Carrie ran laughing into the wrong corners at first, but she soon learned.

They all ran till they were gasping from running and shouting and laughing. They had to rest, and Ma said, 'Bring me the slate and I'll tell you a story.'

'Why do you need a slate to tell a story?' Laura asked as she laid the slate in Ma's lap.

'You'll see,' said Ma, and she told this story:

Far in the woods there was a pond, like this:

The pond was full of fishes, like this:

Down below the pond lived two home-steaders, each in a little tent, because they had not built their houses yet:

They went often to the pond to fish, and they made crooked paths:

A little way from the pond lived an old man and an old woman in a little house with a window:

One day the old woman went to the pond to get a pail of water:

And she saw the fishes all flying out of the pond, like this:

The old woman ran back as fast as she could go, to tell the old man, 'All the fishes are flying out of the pond!' The old man stuck his long nose out of the house to have a good look:

And he said: 'Pshaw! It's nothing but tadpoles!'

'It's a bird!' Carrie yelled, and she clapped her hands and laughed till she rolled off the footstool. Laura and Mary laughed too and coaxed, 'Tell us another, Ma! Please!'

'Well, if I must,' said Ma, and she began, 'This is the house that Jack built for two pieces of money.'

She covered both sides of the slate with the pictures of that story. Ma let Mary and Laura read it and look at the pictures as long as they liked. Then she asked, 'Mary, can you tell that story?'

'Yes!' Mary answered.

Ma wiped the slate clean and gave it to Mary. 'Write it on the slate, then,' she said. 'And Laura and Carrie, I have new playthings for you.'

She gave her thimble to Laura, and Mary's thimble to Carrie, and she showed them that pressing the thimbles into the frost on the windows made perfect circles. They could make pictures on the windows.

With thimble-circles Laura made a Christmas tree. She made birds flying. She made a log house with smoke coming out of the chimney. She even made a roly-poly man and a roly-poly woman. Carrie made just circles.

When Laura finished her window and Mary looked up from the slate, the room was dusky. Ma smiled at them.

'We have been so busy we forgot all about dinner,' she said. 'Come eat your suppers now.'

'Don't you have to do the chores first?' Laura asked.

'Not tonight,' said Ma. 'It was so late when I fed the stock this morning that I gave them enough to last till tomorrow. Maybe the storm will not be so bad then.'

All at once Laura felt miserable. So did Mary. And Carrie whimpered, 'I want Pa!'

'Hush, Carrie!' Ma said, and Carrie hushed.

'We must not worry about Pa,' Ma said, firmly. She

lighted the lamp, but she did not set it in the window. 'Come eat your suppers now,' she said again, 'and then we'll all go to bed.'

39

The Third Day

All night the house shook and jarred in the wind. Next day the storm was worse than ever. The noises of the wind were more terrible and snow struck the windows with an icy rattle.

Ma made ready to go to the stable. 'Eat your breakfast, girls, and be careful with the fire,' she said. Then she was gone into the storm.

After a long time she came back and another day began.

It was a dark, long day. They huddled close to the stove and the cold pressed against their backs. Carrie was fretful, and Ma's smile was tired. Laura and Mary studied hard, but they did not know their lessons very well. The hands of the clock moved so slowly that they seemed not to move at all.

At last the grey light faded away and night was there again. The lamplight shone on the board walls and the white-frosted windows. If Pa had been there he would have played the fiddle and they would all have been cosy and happy.

'Come, come!' Ma said. 'We mustn't sit like this. Would you like to play cat's cradle?'

Jack had left his supper untouched. He sighed mournfully in his corner. Mary and Laura looked at each other, and then Laura said: 'No, thank you, Ma. We want to go to bed.'

She cuddled her back tight against Mary's back in the icy-cold bed. The storm was shaking the house; it creaked and shuddered all over. Rattling snow scoured the roof. Laura's head was tucked well under the covers, but the sounds in the storm were worse than wolves. Cold tears ran down her cheeks.

40

The Fourth Day

In the morning those sounds were gone from the wind. It was blowing with a steady wailing scream and the house stood still. But the roaring fire in the stove gave hardly any heat.

'The cold is worse,' Ma said. 'Don't try to do the housework properly. Wrap up in your shawls and keep Carrie with you close to the stove.'

Soon after Ma came back from the stable, the frost on the eastern window glowed faintly yellow. Laura ran to breathe on it and scratched away the ice until she made a peep-hole. Outdoors the sun was shining!

Ma looked out, then Mary and Laura took turns looking out at the snow blowing in waves over the ground. The sky looked like ice. Even the air looked cold above that fast-blowing flood of snow, and the sunshine that came through the peep-hole was no warmer than a shadow.

Sidewise from the peep-hole, Laura glimpsed something dark. A furry big animal was wading deep in the blowing snow. A bear, she thought. It shambled behind the corner of the house and darkened the front window.

'Ma!' she cried. The door opened, the snowy, furry animal came in. Pa's eyes looked out of its face. Pa's voice said, 'Have you been good girls while I was gone?'

Ma ran to him. Laura and Mary and Carrie ran, crying and laughing. Ma helped him out of his coat. The fur was full of snow that showered on the floor. Pa let the coat drop, too.

'Charles! You're frozen!' Ma said.

'Just about,' said Pa. 'And I'm hungry as a wolf. Let me sit down by the fire, Caroline, and feed me.'

His face was thin and his eyes large. He sat shivering, close to the oven, and said he was only cold, not frostbitten. Ma quickly warmed some of the bean broth and gave it to him.

'That's good,' he said. 'That warms a fellow.'

Ma pulled off his boots and he put his feet up to the heat from the oven.

'Charles,' Ma asked, 'did you – Were you –' She stood smiling with her mouth trembling.

'Now, Caroline, don't you ever worry about me,' said Pa. 'I'm bound to come home to take care of you and the girls.' He lifted Carrie to his knee, and put an arm around Laura, and the other around Mary. 'What did you think, Mary?'

'I thought you would come,' Mary answered.

'That's the girl! And you, Laura?'

'I didn't think you were with Mr Fitch telling stories,' said Laura. 'I – I kept wishing hard.'

'There you are, Caroline! How could a fellow fail to get home?' Pa asked Ma. 'Give me some more of that broth, and I'll tell you all about it.'

They waited while he rested, and ate bean broth with bread, and drank hot tea. His hair and his beard were wet with snow melting in them. Ma dried them with a towel. He took her hand and drew her down beside him and asked:

'Caroline, do you know what this weather means? It means we'll have a bumper crop of wheat next year!'

'Does it, Charles?' said Ma.

'We won't have any grasshoppers next summer. They say in town that grasshoppers come only when the summers are hot and dry and the winters are mild. We are getting so much snow now that we're bound to have fine crops next year.'

'That's good, Charles,' Ma said, quietly.

'Well, they were talking about all this in the store, but I knew I ought to start home. Just as I was leaving, Fitch showed me the buffalo coat. He got it cheap from a man who went east on the last train running, and had to have money to buy his ticket. Fitch said I could have the coat for ten dollars. Ten dollars is a lot of money, but –'

'I'm glad you got the coat, Charles,' said Ma.

'As it turned out, it's lucky I did, though I didn't know it then. But going to town, the wind went right through me. It was cold enough to freeze the nose off a brass monkey. And seemed like my old coat didn't even strain that wind. So when Fitch told me to pay him when I sell my trapped furs next spring, I put that buffalo coat on over my old one.

'As soon as I was out on the prairie I saw the cloud in the north-west, but it was so small and far away that I thought I could beat it home. Pretty soon I began to run, but I was no more than half-way when the storm struck me. I couldn't see my hand before my face.

'It would be all right if these blizzard winds didn't come from all directions at once. I don't know how they do it. When a storm comes from the north-west, a man ought to be able to go straight north by keeping the wind on his left cheek. But a fellow can't do anything like that in a blizzard.

'Still, it seemed I ought to be able to walk straight ahead, even if I couldn't see or tell directions. So I kept on walking, straight ahead, I thought. Till I knew I was lost. I had come a good two miles without getting to the creek, and I had no idea which way to turn. The only thing to do was to keep on going. I had to walk till the storm quit. If I stopped I'd freeze.

'So I set myself to outwalk the storm. I walked and walked. I could not see any more than if I had been stone blind. I could hear nothing but the wind. I kept on walking in that white blur. I don't know if you noticed, there seem to be voices howling and things screaming overhead, in a blizzard?'

'Yes, Pa, I heard them!' Laura said.

'So did I,' said Mary. And Ma nodded.

'And balls of fire,' said Laura.

'Balls of fire?' Pa asked.

'That will keep, Laura,' said Ma. 'Go on, Charles. What did you do?'

'I kept on walking,' Pa answered. 'I walked till the white blur turned grey and then black, and I knew it was night. I figured I had been walking four hours, and these blizzards last three days and nights. But I kept on walking.'

Pa stopped, and Ma said, 'I had the lamp burning in the window for you.'

'I didn't see it,' said Pa. 'I kept straining my eyes to see something, but all I saw was the dark. Then of a sudden, everything gave way under me and I went straight down, must have been ten feet. It seemed farther.

'I had no idea what had happened or where I was. But I was out of the wind. The blizzard was yelling and shrieking overhead, but the air was fairly still where I was. I felt around me. There was snow banked up as high as I could reach on three sides of me, and the other side was a kind of wall of bare ground, sloping back at the bottom.

'It didn't take me long to figure that I'd walked off the bank of some gully, somewhere on the prairie. I crawled back under the bank, and there I was with solid ground at my back and overhead, snug as a bear in a den. I didn't believe I would freeze there, out of the wind and with the buffalo coat to keep warmth in my body. So I curled up in it and went to sleep, being pretty tired.

'My, I was glad I had that coat, and a good warm cap with earflaps, and that extra pair of thick socks, Caroline.

'When I woke up I could hear the blizzard, but faintly. There was solid snow in front of me, coated over with ice where my breath had melted it. The blizzard had filled up the hole I had made when I fell. There must have been six feet of snow over me, but the air was good. I moved my arms and legs and fingers and toes, and felt my nose and ears to make sure I was not freezing. I could still hear the storm, so I went to sleep again.

'How long has it been, Caroline?'

'Three days and nights,' said Ma. 'This is the fourth day.'

Then Pa asked Mary and Laura, 'Do you know what day this is?'

'Is it Sunday?' Mary guessed.

'It's the day before Christmas,' said Ma.

Laura and Mary had forgotten all about Christmas. Laura asked, 'Did you sleep all that time, Pa?'

'No,' said Pa. 'I kept on sleeping and waking up hungry, and sleeping some more, till I woke up just about starved. I was bringing home some oyster crackers for Christmas. They were in a pocket of the buffalo coat. I took a handful of those crackers out of the paper bag and ate them. I felt out in the snow and took a handful, and I ate that for a drink. Then all I could do was lie there and wait for the storm to stop.

'I tell you, Caroline, it was mighty hard to do that, thinking of you and the girls and knowing you would go out in the blizzard to do the chores. But I knew I could not get home till the blizzard stopped.

'So I waited a long time, till I was so hungry again that I ate all the rest of the oyster crackers. They were no bigger than the end of my thumb. One of them wasn't half a mouthful, and the whole half-pound of them wasn't very filling.

'Then I went on waiting, sleeping some. I guessed it was night again. Whenever I woke I listened closely, and I could hear the dim sound of the blizzard. I could tell by that sound that the snow was getting thicker over me, but the air was still good in my den. The heat of my blood was keeping me from freezing.

'I tried to sleep all I could, but I was so hungry that I kept waking up. Finally I was too hungry to sleep at all.

Girls, I was bound and determined I would not do it, but after some time I did. I took the paper bag out of the inside pocket of my old overcoat, and I ate every bit of the Christmas candy. I'm sorry.'

Laura hugged him from one side and Mary hugged him from the other. They hugged him hard and Laura said, 'Oh Pa, I am so glad you did!'

'So am I, Pa! So am I!' said Mary. They were truly glad.

'Well,' Pa said, 'we'll have a big wheat crop next year, and you girls won't have to wait till next Christmas for candy.'

'Was it good, Pa?' Laura asked. 'Did you feel better after you ate it?'

'It was very good, and I felt much better,' said Pa. 'I went right to sleep and I must have slept most of yesterday and last night. Suddenly I sat up wide awake. I could not hear a sound.

'Now, was I buried so deep in snow that I couldn't hear the blizzard, or had it stopped? I listened hard. It was so still that I could hear the silence.

'Girls, I began digging on that snow like a badger. I wasn't slow in digging up out of that den. I came scrabbling through the top of that snow bank, and where do you suppose I was?

'I was on the bank of Plum Creek, just above the

place where we set the fish-trap, Laura.'

'Why, I can see that place from the window,' said Laura.

'Yes. And I could see this house,' said Pa. All that long, terrible time he had been so near. The lamp in the window had not been able to shine into the blizzard at all, or he would have seen its light.

'My legs were so stiff and cramped that I could hardly stand on them,' said Pa. 'But I saw this house and I started for home just as fast as I could go. And here I am!' he finished, hugging Laura and Mary.

Then he went to the big buffalo coat and he took out of one of its pockets a flat, square-edge can of bright tin. He asked, 'What do you think I have brought you for Christmas dinner?'

They could not guess.

'Oysters!' said Pa. 'Nice, fresh oysters! They were frozen solid when I got them, and they are frozen solid yet. Better put them in the lean-to, Caroline, so they will stay that way till tomorrow.'

Laura touched the can. It was cold as ice.

'I ate up the oyster crackers, and I ate up the Christmas candy, but by jinks,' said Pa, 'I brought the oysters home!'

41

Christmas Eve

Pa went early to do the chores that evening, and Jack went with him, staying close to his heels. Jack did not intend to lose sight of Pa again.

They came in, cold and snowy. Pa stamped the snow from his feet and hung his old coat with his cap on the nail by the lean-to door. 'The wind is rising again,' he said. 'We will have another blizzard before morning.'

'Just so you are here, Charles, I don't care how much it storms,' said Ma.

Jack lay down contentedly and Pa sat warming his hands by the stove.

'Laura,' he said, 'if you'll bring me the fiddle-box I'll play you a tune.'

Laura brought the fiddle-box to him. Pa tuned the fiddle and rosined the bow, and then while Ma cooked supper he filled the house with music.

> 'Oh, Charley he's a fine young man,
>   Oh, Charley he's a dandy!
> Charley likes to kiss the girls

And he can do it handy!

'I don't want none of your weevily wheat,
   I don't want none of your barley,
I want fine flour in half an hour,
   To bake a cake for Charley!'

Pa's voice rollicked with the rollicking tune, and Carrie laughed and clapped her hands, and Laura's feet were dancing.

Then the fiddle changed the tune and Pa began to sing about Lily Dale.

''Twas a calm, still night,
And the moon's pale light
Shone soft o'er hill and dale . . .'

Pa glanced at Ma, busy at the stove, while Mary and Laura sat listening, and the fiddle slipped into frolicking up and down with his voice.

'Mary put the dishes on,
The dishes on, the dishes on,
Mary put the dishes on,
We'll all take tea!'

'And what shall I do, Pa?' Laura cried, while Mary ran to get the plates and cups from the cupboard. The fiddle and Pa kept singing, down all the steps they had just gone up.

> 'Laura take them off again,
> Off again, off again,
> Laura clear the table when
> We've all gone away!'

So Laura knew that Mary was to set the table for supper and she was to clear away afterwards.

The wind was screaming fiercer and louder outside. Snow whirled swish-swishing against the windows. But Pa's fiddle sang in the warm, lamplighted house. The dishes made small clinking sounds as Mary set the table. Carrie rocked herself in the rocking-chair and Ma went gently between the table and the stove. In the middle of the table she set a milk-pan full of beautiful brown baked beans, and now from the oven she took the square baking-pan full of golden corn-bread. The rich brown smell and the sweet golden smell curled deliciously together in the air.

Pa's fiddle laughed and sang,

'I'm Captain Jinks of the Horse Marines,
I feed my horse on corn and beans
Although 'tis far beyond my means, for
I'm Captain Jinks of the Horse Marines!
I'm Captain of the army!'

Laura patted Jack's furry smooth forehead and scratched his ears for him, and then with both hands she gave his head a quick, happy squeeze. Everything was so good. Grasshoppers were gone, and next year Pa could harvest the wheat. Tomorrow was Christmas, with oyster stew for dinner. There would be no presents and no candy, but Laura could not think of anything she wanted and she was so glad that the Christmas candy had helped to bring Pa safe home again.

'Supper is ready,' Ma said in her gentle voice.

Pa laid the fiddle in its box. He stood up and looked around at them all. His blue eyes shone at them.

'Look, Caroline,' he said, 'how Laura's eyes are shining.'

Discover more titles in the Little House series, based on the real childhood adventures of *Laura Ingalls Wilder*

Little House in the Big Woods

Inside the cosy little house in the
Big Woods lives the Ingalls family:
Ma, Pa, Mary, Laura and baby Carrie.
Outside the little house, in the snow
and the cold, are the wild animals.

This is the classic tale of how they live together,
mostly in harmony, but sometimes in fear . . .

Little House
on the Prairie

The sun-kissed prairie stretches out around
the Ingalls family, smiling its welcome after
their long, hard journey across America.

But looks can be deceiving, and they soon
find that they must share the land with
wild bears and Indians.

Will there be enough land for all of them?

The Hundred and One Dalmatians

By Dodie Smith

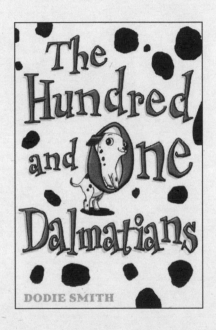

Cruella de Vil is enough to frighten the spots off a Dalmatian pup. But when she steals a whole family of them, the puppies' parents, Pongo and Missus, lose no time in mounting a daring rescue mission.

Will they be in time to thwart Cruella's evil scheme, or have they bitten off more than they can chew?